<u>BOOK PRIZE</u>

Awarded to:
ANNE MARIE HOGAN,
PRESENTATION N.S.
Tipperary County Library

Cold Marble

ff

COLD
MARBLE
and other ghost stories

Catherine Storr

faber and faber
LONDON . BOSTON

First published in 1985
by Faber and Faber Limited
3 Queen Square London WC1N 3AU
Reprinted in 1986

Filmset by Wilmaset Birkenhead Wirral
Printed in Great Britain by
Butler and Tanner Frome Somerset

British Library Cataloguing in Publication Data
Storr, Catherine
Cold marble: and other ghost stories.
I. Title
823′.914[J]   PZ7
ISBN 0–571–13582–x

CONTENTS

Acknowledgements

The Boy's Story by Catherine Storr appeared in *The Methuen Book of Strange Tales* edited by Jean Russell, published by Methuen Children's Books. *Bill's Ghost* by Catherine Storr appeared in *Ghosts and Shadows*, edited by Dorothy Edwards, published by Lutterworth Press.

Cold Marble

Years before Julie came to live there, the great Victorian house had been divided up, quite cleverly, into small self-contained flats. Where there had once been a wide stairway leading up from the ground floor to the vast first floor drawing-room, there was now a narrow flight of steep steps, saving space so that more little rooms could be carved out of half-landings and wide corridors. The blind ends of passages became cramped little kitchens or bathrooms with artificial ventilation and light. The big rooms were all cut up and partitioned, so that some became the whole of one or even two new flats. Julie's, on the second floor, was one of these. It was really no more than one long, narrow room in which she lived and slept, with a tiny kitchen in a sort of cupboard, and the smallest bathroom she had ever seen. A thin dividing wall had been run down the middle of the old room, separating Julie's flatlet from Miss Boden's next door. The wall not only split the big room in half, it had also, unavoidably, cut into two the great marble mantelpiece on the wall opposite the window. The fireplace had been boarded up with white plaster board which looked bare and modern and mean beside the festoons of carved fruit and leaves which decorated the surrounding marble. Julie's small, two-bar electric fire, placed under the generous mantelshelf, was a poor substitute for the real flames which must once have danced in the grate. In spite of this, Julie thought her half mantelpiece was odd and funny, and she liked it.

But she was lonely. She had left her home in the North to get away from her father's second wife, with whom she had nothing in common, and had come to London to share a flat with a school friend, who had also found her a job. A month after Julie arrived in London, the friend met, and almost immediately married, a Canadian and left the country with him. She was apologetic, but sure that now Julie was in the big city she wouldn't want to go back to village life. Julie didn't. But she found London strange and vast and indifferent, and though she'd often resented the curiosity her village neighbours had shown about her private life, she would have welcomed a little interest shown by anyone she met now. The other people in her office were a good deal older than she was and seemed to be already locked into their own private lives, with no room for a new acquaintance. When Julie had left the too expensive flat she had shared with Aggie and had moved into the big house, she had hoped that one or two of the other tenants might become friends. But it hadn't turned out like that. She saw so little of any of them that she was never sure whether the people she occasionally passed on the stairs were living in the house, or were visitors. Miss Boden, next door to her, was out a great deal and away for most weekends. She was polite, but not warm. On the one occasion when Julie had knocked on her door and asked if she could borrow half a cup of milk, Miss Boden had obliged; but her generosity in giving Julie the full half pint carton, and insisting that it was not a loan but a gift, made it clear that she did not want Julie to knock on her door again.

Because she was lonely, she liked trying to imagine the

people who had lived in the big house in the last century, when it had been the home of one family, people who belonged to each other. She felt that she didn't belong to anyone. As she had no name for them, she thought of them as Ther Family. Mr and Mrs Ther Family, and, of course, children. Perhaps an unmarried sister, or an old aunt tucked away on an upper floor, not entitled to quite all the privileges of her hosts. As she went up and down the mean stairs, Julie pictured the place as it had been; there would be a thick carpet on the broad steps, held in place by polished brass stair-rods. There would be daylight pouring through the wide windows, framed by heavy curtains, fastened back by glistening silk rope. The doors that led to the large rooms would be of shining mahogany, with deeply carved panels and heavy handles and locks. Probably maids in caps and aprons had trudged up those stairs, carrying bright copper cans of hot water to the gentry in the grand bedrooms on the upper floors. Then they would have come down again with the empty cans and damp towels, back to the dark and beetly basement; today it was called 'the lower ground floor', but it was still dark and probably still beetly. Down there, below stairs, as they used to say, there would have been a fat cook, a kitchen maid, perhaps a boy whose job was to clean boots and shoes. Up here, on the second floor, a lady's maid, very proper in black silk, mending her mistress's clothes and arranging her hair for parties. There would also be a nurse and a nursemaid who would look after the baby and the next one or two children up; on the floor above, she imagined a schoolroom, with a bony, dissatisfied gover-ness, probably French or German and a long way from home, as Julie was herself. She wouldn't think too much about that. She preferred to people the house with comfortable Mr and Mrs Ther Family, with their rosy, loved children, and with an imaginary domestic staff who enjoyed their work and were well treated, and who had been here so long, they were almost like friends or relations. It must have been lovely, Julie thought, to have been one of that household; best of all to belong to Ther Family, and to have been able to lie in bed in the whole big room of which she now had half, and to be woken in the morning by one of the friendly maids coming in with kindling and a bucket of coals, to light the fire in the huge grate so that the place was really warm before she had to get up and dress. Even if she nipped out of bed the moment she woke, her mingy little two-bar electric fire never managed to do more than take the chill off the end of the room nearest it.

It was a cool, damp autumn, and it drew gradually into a bitter winter. Julie had caught a sort of flu that had been going round the office, and she didn't seem able to shake it off. One of the women bosses told her she ought to ask her doctor if he couldn't give her something to stop her coughing, and Julie said she would. She didn't, because she had never yet got round to registering with one of the local general practices. She tried to stifle the cough when the woman boss was around, but she knew that really it wasn't getting any better. It was exhausting, too; when she reached her flatlet in the evenings, all she wanted to do was to crawl into bed and to try to get warm enough to sleep. She was too tired to cook, she bought frozen dinners, but often she was too tired to eat them. She knew that she'd lost quite a lot of weight, her skirts were loose, and the cords she wore at week-ends nearly dropped off her. The woman boss told her she should go home for the Christmas break and get her Mum to fatten her up. She meant it kindly, but at the word 'Mum', Julie's throat tightened and her eyes pricked, and all she could say was that of course she would do just that. Her real Mum had died when she was five. She didn't fancy going on the long journey north to the casual welcome she knew she'd get from her Mum's successor. She thought, 'I'll stay in the flat. I'll keep the electric fire on all day. I'll feed myself up, I'll stop in bed. Then I'll be better.'

Two days before Christmas Day, when the holiday period began, Julie was let out of the office early. She arrived home to find what seemed like everyone leaving. Two unknown characters passed her as she went upstairs, and after she'd shut her own door behind her, she could hear other feet tramping down the stairway, and the bump, bump, bump of heavy luggage being dragged behind the footsteps. By eight o'clock that evening the house was quiet, and it was then that Julie realized how many small sounds of other people's ordinary lives she usually heard and found comforting; they had told her that she was not entirely alone. Now the silence pressed on her ear-drums. And it was a bitterly cold silence. Until this evening she had not understood how much warmth one small flatlet gained from the little areas of heat generated in the neighbouring flats. Now that hers was the only fire in the building, she knew just how hopeless those two short red bars were. Her room was icy. She piled on pullovers and cardigans, she made herself innumerable cups of tea, but she could not get warm.

It was a relief to give up the struggle. She filled a hot-water bottle and went to bed. But in the night the fever she'd been running for the last week or so returned. She was too hot. Then she was cold again. She knew she ought to get out of bed to turn off the light and the fire, but her legs felt trembly and she stayed where she was, neither quite asleep nor quite awake. She thought she must be dreaming when the marble of her half mantelpiece looked flushed rosy with a changing light, she heard footsteps, voices. But when she opened her heavy eyes to look properly, there was no one there, and the white marble was only faintly tinged with the steady orange of the electric fire. The house was dead silent all around her. She pulled the blankets further up and tried to sleep again. Probably she'd feel better tomorrow.

Tomorrow was Christmas Eve, and she didn't feel better. She made an unsteady journey to the bathroom, made more tea and filled another hot-water bottle, then crept back to bed. She had her radio by her, and she listened at intervals, during the long, dark day, to Christmas programmes of general jollity or carol-singing. Sometimes, in her confused state, she thought she heard a child's voice joining in a hymn or a carol, as if the singer was in the room with her. Once, as she woke from a short sleep, she thought she saw the flick of a white skirt passing her bed. Towards evening she fell into a more profound sleep, and when she woke she felt different. Not so feverish, somehow lighter, more at ease. But the room she woke into was strange, she didn't recognize it. She wondered if she had been much worse than she'd known, and that somehow she'd been transported to a hospital, to be nursed there. But it wasn't like any hospital room she'd ever seen. It was large and square, with a patterned wallpaper and pictures hanging, one above another, on the walls. There were thick curtains drawn across the window. There was a big open fire, and the flames that leapt in the grate were reflected back from the shining surfaces of mahogany furniture with twinkling brass handles. Against one wall stood three beds; one was short, a child's bed, one was long, the third was a cot with barred sides. In the big bed lay the form of a sleeping adult, in the cot was the hunched bundle of a baby. But in the short bed a small girl in a frilled nightgown sat upright and looked at Julie with wide-open eyes.

'Are you a ghost?' the child asked.

Another dream. But this time, quite a pleasant one. Because, even in a dream, you mustn't frighten a child, she said, 'Of course not. I'm an ordinary person. Like you.'

'If you're not a ghost, how did you get here?' the child asked.

'I'm not sure. I don't even know where this is,' Julie said.

'It's our night-nursery. That's Nurse. She's asleep just now. But if she wakes up and sees you, she'll probably scream. She's frightened of ghosts.'

'But I'm not . . .' Julie had begun, when she interrupted herself. 'That's my mantelpiece there! Only you've got the whole of it. Then it is my room! Or half of it's mine.' She felt that she wasn't making sense, but the child was perfectly composed.

'It isn't your room yet. If it was your room, then I'd be the ghost,' she said. As she spoke, the walls of the room began to waver and dissolve, like a reflection in water which has been troubled. The solid-looking furniture, the pictures, the curtains, trembled and faded. She was looking at the bare distempered walls of her own room. She saw the khaki-coloured linoleum on the floor. The firelight dimmed, the half mantelpiece was greyish white. She shivered. But the child was there, standing by her bed, still looking at her intently, with those large dark eyes.

'You see? When it's your room, I'm the ghost.'

'And when it's your night-nursery?' Julie said, playing along with a game she didn't understand.

'Then it's your turn to be the ghost. You go backwards and I go forwards, that's all the difference. When it's *Now* for you, I can come forwards and ghost you. When it's my Now, you come back to ghost me.'

The walls of the room trembled again, and it seemed to Julie that she could see both rooms at once, like the negatives of two photographs superimposed on the same piece of film. She saw the narrow divan bed in which she had been lying, and she saw also the white counterpanes on the Nurse's and the child's beds in that other room. She saw the meagre length of brown curtain hanging over her own window and the trellised pattern of the ample curtains in that other room. She heard the faint voice of her radio, which she'd forgotten to switch off, and she heard, distantly, the repeated call of a cuckoo clock sounding more often than she could count. She saw her own empty mantelshelf above the blocked-in grate, and she saw the length of warmed marble in the night-nursery, loaded with ornaments: two vases, a china figure, a picture in a silver frame. From the shelf hung three stockings, one long, one shorter, one a baby's bootee.

'It's Christmas tomorrow,' the child said, seeing what Julie was looking at.

'Happy Christmas, then,' Julie said.

'Is it Christmas in your Now? You haven't hung up your stocking.'

'I'm too old,' Julie said.

'I don't suppose you're older than Nurse. That's her stocking there. That was my last Christmas,' the child said, and now she was standing again in Julie's room, and Julie found that she was standing too, by the child's side.

'What do you mean, your last Christmas?' she asked.

'I mean I wasn't there for the next one.'

'You . . .' Julie didn't want to use the word, but the child was quite direct. 'I died that Spring. That's why I'm like I am when I'm ghosting you. I never grew more than this.' She held out a hand at the level of the top of her head to show what she meant.

'So if you're a ghost, you stay the same age you were when you . . .'

'When you died. You'll get used to saying it,' the child consoled her.

'But then . . . other ghosts can't be the same as when you knew them here.' Julie felt confused.

'No, they aren't. My mamma's ghost is younger than my sister's. We all think that's very funny,' the child said. Behind her the marble glowed rosy again, and the shapes of furniture loomed and retreated. Julie saw the baby stir in its cot, then settle itself again with a tiny murmur of content. Then the warm light dimmed and she was back in her own room. The child was still there.

A new thought struck her. She said, 'You said when this was your room I came back to ghost you. But I'm not a ghost. I'm there, asleep in my own bed. I'm dreaming.' Indeed she could see herself, lying very straight and quiet in her bed.

The child did not answer. She continued to stare at Julie, with that not unfriendly, faintly curious look. This made Julie look down at herself. She was half afraid she'd see nothing, that she was invisible, since there was her sleeping body on the bed, and that would mean that the child was right and she was a ghost. But she was reassured by what she saw. She was there, dressed in her ordinary clothes, standing on her familiar feet. She said, 'You told me ghosts were the same age as they'd been when they were people and died. But I'm just like I am now . . .'

The child nodded gravely. 'That's right. You'll never look any different from how you are now.'

'Then I'm . . . What are you doing here?' Julie cried out, ready to be angry at what seemed a bad joke, or even a plan to frighten her. But the child was not disturbed. She said, 'I was sent to fetch you. Shall we go?'

Cold Marble

She held out her hand, and Julie took it. The small fingers curled about hers. They were as cold as the white marble of the mantelpiece, but Julie did not shiver at the touch. Hers were cold too.

The Boy's Story

'Tell me a ghost story,' the boy said.

'I don't know any,' the father answered.

'Haven't you ever seen a ghost?' the boy asked.

'Of course I haven't.'

'Don't you know anyone who's seen a ghost?'

'No.'

'How do you know? Someone might have seen a ghost and you didn't know about it.'

'People I know don't see ghosts. They're not the sort,' the father said.

'What sort of people do see ghosts, then?' the boy persisted.

'Don't know. Weird people. Not anyone like you or me.'

The boy sighed. If ordinary people didn't see ghosts, then where were the ghosts? Who did see them? Where did ghost stories come from? He tried again.

'If you did see a ghost, right now – what would you do?'

'Now? In the middle of the town, in daylight?'

'It's not all that daylight now. Anyway, suppose you were here and it was dark and you saw a ghost, what would you do?'

'How would I know it was a ghost?' the father asked. He was a practical man.

'You'd know,' the boy said, confident.

'I wouldn't take any notice of it.'

'Suppose it started to come after you?'

'If I wasn't taking any notice of it, I wouldn't know it was coming after me, would I?'

'You'd feel it coming. Not running. Just walking, slowly.'

'Where is this ghost when I see it first?' the father asked, humouring his son.

The boy considered. He looked around the crowded street. He looked at the bright shop windows, sprinkled with imitation frost and bright with crimson and gold for the Christmas season. He looked at the cars massed too closely to move faster than he could walk. He tried to imagine the street dark, deserted, silent. Difficult, when now it was all bustle and glitter and people, laden with gaily wrapped parcels, pushing past. At night it would be another world.

He saw that the entrance of the occasional shop was set back from the pavement, flanked by the brilliantly-lit display windows. Now there were people pushing in and out of the doors and window-shopping on their way in. But when the shops were closed and the people gone, those hollowed passages would be shadowed, mysterious. He pointed.

'There. You see It standing there.' He could almost see It himself. The light from the overhead street lamps would not reach right up to the shuttered doorway.

His father was not looking at the pointing finger. 'In the street?' he said, and laughed.

'In the doorway. You don't notice it at first. Not until you're walking past, like we are now. And then you feel.'

'Feel? What?'

'Something. Cold.'

'It is cold,' the father said.

'And you look, sort of sideways. Without turning your head, because you don't want It to think you're really looking. But you do see It. Just standing. It doesn't move, not then. But you know It's watching you.'

'I suppose it's wearing armour? Has its head under its arm? Something like that?' the father said, prepared to play along.

'That'd be silly. Anyway, you don't see it properly. Remember, it's dark in there. And you're only looking sideways, not straight at It. You don't know exactly what It looks like. You just have this feeling. You know It's there because of you. Waiting for you.'

'I'd go back and take a proper look,' the father said.

'No, you wouldn't!'

'Why not?'

'Because you're frightened. You don't want to go back. You want to get away as quickly as you can.'

'We'd get on a lot quicker if it wasn't for this crowd,' the father said, only half listening to the boy.

'The street'd be empty then. And you'd be listening.'

'Listening? What for?'

'The footsteps.'

'What footsteps? You said there wouldn't be anyone else around.'

'*Its* footsteps. What you hope you didn't see.'

'Running after me?'

'Not running, walking. Like you are, not any faster. So you can't be sure you're really hearing them, because they're keeping time with you. If you stop, It stops too. So you can't be sure,' the boy repeated.

'I should turn round and have a look. That'd be the sensible thing to do.'

'You aren't feeling sensible,' the boy said.

His father was bored with the game. He said, 'Hungry?

21

What about some tea? They have crumpets at Jerninghams. We have to go there, anyway, to get the gear your Mum needs for icing the cake.'

The restaurant in the big shop was on the fifth floor. Sitting high above the sparkling streets, they drank hot sweet brown tea, and sucked the salty butter out of crumpets full of holes. At last, pleasantly full, they were borne down in the lift to the basement for Mum's kitchen gadgets. It took a little time to find exactly the icing nozzle she had specified, and when they reached the street again it was dark and the street lamps were lit. The red rear lights of the cars backed away from them, like the eyes of cowed animals. Far above them, difficult to see against the glare of fluorescent light, the sky was pierced by a few pinpricks of stars.

'Where do we go now?' the boy asked. The heat of the big shop had made him sleepy, and his legs ached. He wouldn't mind going home straight away. There were Christmas preparations he had still to make.

'Got to get a bit of wood, fifty-four by ninety by five for the shelf in the larder. Half a dozen cup-hooks, and a couple of screws. Might as well call in and see if Dockers have got that beading I asked them for. That's all,' the father said.

They had to walk further along the crowded street, and then there was a long wait while the piece of wood, fifty-four by ninety by five, was found. It was nearly an hour later that father and son came out into the street again and made their way back towards the bus station. In that hour everything had changed. The other shoppers had gone, the shops were closed. The scene had an empty, deserted look, which was somehow exaggerated by the torn scraps of coloured paper, tinsel, empty sweet cartons and even the wrinkled skin of a dead balloon. It was colder. The father turned up his coat collar and shivered.

The Boy's Story

Although the crowds which had held them up before were gone, the father and son walked slowly, the father lumbered with the piece of wood, the boy because he was tired. He lagged behind, and his father called to him sharply. 'Get a move on, son. We don't want to be here all night.'

'I'm coming as fast as I can,' the boy said.

The father waited for the boy to catch up with him, but two minutes later he had fallen behind again. His father half turned his head to remonstrate. As he turned, his eye was caught by the front of the shop he was just about to pass. It seemed vaguely familiar, and he glanced up to read the name above the entrance but, by some trick of light, the silvered surface of the lettering reflected the crossed beams of the street lamps with such dazzling power that for a moment he seemed blinded. His gaze dropped to the shop's doorway, set far back between two shrouded windows. It was dark in there, black dark. Was it because his eyes had just been insulted by that reflected glare from the panel above that the darkness seemed more intense, the shadows more threatening than in the other badly lit parts of the street? His feet, by this time, had carried him almost past the entrance. For some reason he didn't want to turn his head to look again. His eyes shifted sideways for reassurance that there was nobody standing far back in the doorway, nothing to be frightened of. Of course he wasn't frightened, there could be nothing there.

What happened next was not reasonable, it was the impulse of blind panic. He found himself running. The wood for the shelving bumped uncomfortably against his side, the carrier bag swung against his knees. With his free hand he had clutched the boy's wrist and he was forcing him to run too. His breath came in short painful gasps, his blood thundered in his ears; but as well as the drumming

23

pulse, he heard the sound of footsteps echoing on the pavement. They might have been his own or the boy's. He couldn't tell if there was a third set, matching theirs, pace for pace, in the empty street behind him.

He checked himself at the corner, where the deserted shopping street met another, wider road, still busy with traffic and belated shoppers. The bus station was less than twenty yards away, and the father saw the comforting shape of the double decker waiting for them, with the heads of other passengers visible through the windows above and below. He shifted the shelving, let go of the boy's wrist, and began walking deliberately towards this haven of safety.

'You hurt me! You've pulled my arm out of its socket,' the boy complained.

'Thought we were going to miss the bus,' the father said, trying to recover his dignity.

'There's another at seven,' the boy said, rubbing his shoulder. Then, in a different voice, he said, 'I've lost my sweets. They were on top of the bag. They must've fallen out when you made me run like that.'

'Doesn't matter,' his father said.

'Does matter. They cost thirty p. I'll go back and look . . .'

'We're not going back,' his father said quickly.

'There's plenty of time. Why can't we. . . ?'

'I'll give you the thirty p. Now come on,' the father said.

The boy followed him, wondering, as he often did, at the waywardness of grown-up people. He climbed the stairs to the top deck of the bus and waited for his father, who was stowing away the awkward lengths of wood in the luggage space under the stairs. The father's legs were still trembling as he joined his son. He was glad to sit down. He put the carrier bag on his lap to hide the shaking of his knees.

'If we hadn't caught this bus, we'd have been late for supper,' he said, feeling the need to justify his sudden dash for safety.

'I'm not hungry,' the boy said, remembering the sweet, rubbery flesh of the crumpets in Jerningham's.

Presently the bus ground its gears and inched cleverly out of the bus station. Soon it was beyond the lighted streets of the town, and was pioneering its way along dark country roads. Trees stood up, black skeletons on each side, scratching with long fingers against the upper windows, making the passengers inside draw back instinctively, as if they feared they might be trapped and pulled into the sightless world without. The boy leaned against his father and in his head went over the events of the afternoon. He thought of the smell of the builder's yard where they had waited for the wood. He thought of the tea at Jerningham's and the soppy music that had been relayed from the loud-speakers as they ate. He thought of the fat china pig he had bought for his Mum's Christmas present; he loved its sly smile and he was sure she would love it too. He thought of the sparkling shopping street and he remembered the conversation he and his Dad had had there. He said, sleepily, 'What would you really do if you saw a ghost, Dad?'

He wasn't surprised that his father didn't answer the question directly. Instead he said, 'We had to catch this bus or your Mum would have worried.'

The boy said, 'No, she wouldn't. She'd know nothing could happen to us going Christmas shopping.'

His father didn't answer that at all. The boy repeated, 'Nothing could happen to us, could it, Dad?'

'Of course not. Whatever could happen to us?' his father said.

The Dream House

'What does it mean if you dream about a house?' Laurie asked.

'Don't ask me. I've never been able to make head or tail of any of my dreams,' her father said.

'Do you know, Mum?'

'Some people say the house is you. Or something about you. What sort of house is it?'

'Baba Yaga's house on chicken's legs. Laurie's got skinny little legs like that,' Fergus jeered.

'I haven't! Shut up, anyway. It isn't just one house, there're lots. Well, about four. But they aren't real.'

'Of course not, if they're dream houses . . .'

'No, I mean, they're not houses I've ever been to. When I'm awake. Only when I dream about them, I always know I've been there before. In another dream. And there's always a bit I didn't know was there. A sort of surprise.'

'Sounds quite interesting,' Laurie's mother said.

'What would that mean, Mum? Not knowing about the bit. Sometimes it's just a room, sometimes it's a whole floor.'

'Could be a talent you didn't know you had.'

'You mean, like singing? Or something?'

'Don't tell her that, Mum. Now she's going to see herself as an opera star. Remember the time she was going to be a

26

ballerina? Singing all over the place'd be worse than those terrible exercises,' Fergus said.

'And I'm always walking through them . . .' Laurie began, ignoring her young brother.

'I'm surprised you can wade through the trash if you've been there before. I've never seen anything like the state of your room,' her father said.

'Oh, Dad! That's only till I've finished with the exams. I haven't got time to clear up properly now. Anyway, they aren't untidy in my dreams. Well, not particularly.' She remembered one of the dream houses, standing back among spindly trees from a rutted country lane, which was certainly not in perfect order. But the latest, one she'd so far dreamed of only once, was quite different. She said, 'One of them's really beautiful. Old. And it's got a long gallery.'

No one was listening. Families don't, especially not to the recounting of dreams. But Laurie felt a sort of pride in this house, built of mellow bricks, with long diamond-paned windows. She had seen it first from outside, set against dark yew trees surrounding grass which, by contrast, was an almost hectic green. She had gone in through the porticoed front door, and found herself in a succession of ground-floor rooms, each one leading into the next. This was a characteristic of all of her dream houses; they didn't have passages with doors to the rooms leading off, like ordinary houses, they had these communicating doors from one to the next. Laurie had seen this arrangement in grand stately homes, but she had no idea why her dream houses followed this pattern. When she was in the dream it seemed perfectly natural, just as it seemed natural that the houses were always familiar, and that they belonged to her; they were hers, her very own, as much as her books, her transistor, her clothes, her character, herself.

The houses all had another feature in common. As she'd told her mother, in each of them there was a portion which Laurie had never seen, which she apparently hadn't known about until she was in this particular dream. As she walked about, touching the furniture or the walls with loving recognition, saying to herself with pleasure, 'So I'm here again!', the realization would suddenly come to her that there was a part of this building which she hadn't yet seen. Every time she had the dream, no matter into which house she 'woke', she found herself exclaiming to some shadowy figure with her, 'Look! Rooms I didn't know were there!' As she spoke, she would feel the excitement of being on the verge of discovery, like the unsealing of the entrance to a lost treasure house, or as a diver might feel when, on the sea-bed, he comes across a long-sunk argosy.

'How long is it till you take these wretched exams?' her father was asking, and at the same time her mother said, 'As soon as they're over I'm taking Laurie to have her eyes tested. She's been having too many headaches lately.'

'It's not my eyes, Mum! It's because it's so hot.' She didn't want to have to wear glasses.

''S'trordinary for the end of April,' Laurie's father said.

'And when I was taking 'O' Levels it was freezing. Remember?'

'That's right! Coldest June for fifty years, or something like that.'

'Perhaps it'll be snowing by the end of May,' Fergus suggested.

But the weather didn't change. It remained thundery hot and the headaches became worse. Laurie kept quiet about them. When her mother exclaimed at her heavy eyes and pale cheeks, she admitted that she wasn't sleeping very well; she was worrying about the examinations, she woke early and heard the birds' dawn chorus, hating them for being so carefree. Before she could go to sleep, her tired mind was rehearsing passages out of set books, French irregular verbs and passages of poetry. When at last she fell asleep, she had anxious dreams; she dreamed that she was late for the examination, she found she had read the wrong set books, she couldn't find her clothes, her pen, her papers. What she didn't tell her mother was about her other dreams, the dreams of the latest of her dream houses. Always before, she had looked forward to visiting these houses, she had felt that they were friendly, and there was the wonderful moment when she was on the verge of exploring the unexpected rooms in them. But the house which was haunting her dreams now, though it was beautiful, was not friendly. It had begun to take on the proportions of a nightmare.

In that very first dream, she hadn't had time to discover more than that it was old and impressive, and she had seen a wide staircase sweeping up from the linked rooms on the ground floor to the long gallery above. When the next dream took her there, she had begun to feel the pleasure that a return visit to one of her dream houses had always brought. She had gone up the grand staircase and had walked along the gallery, hung with pictures in heavy, old-fashioned frames. They were all portraits, and Laurie knew, in the mysterious way you do in dreams, that they were portraits of her ancestors. Most of them were women, and all of them were young, some under twenty years old, some not much more. There must have been a tradition, Laurie thought, still dreaming, that the females of the family had their portraits painted before they married; or – since one or two held babies or very small children – very early in their married lives. There were no middle-aged matrons, no grandmothers. Laurie's own grandmother had died before she'd reached her thirtieth birthday; Laurie's mother, her daughter, couldn't remember her mother. Were there any portraits of the men of the family? Laurie couldn't remember, after she'd woken up.

She had woken feeling oppressed, but she put this down to the strain she was under. When she found herself in the same house a night or two later, she was ready to be pleased, but at the same time she was vaguely apprehensive. She walked through the ground floor rooms and ascended the stairs. She walked again along the picture gallery. This time her attention was caught by an irregularity in a panel of dark wood beside one of the paintings. She reached out a hand to a carved linen fold, and found that she had pressed the spring which opened a small door. The door opened towards her and she pulled. Beyond, she saw a flight of narrow, uncarpeted steps, spiralling upwards.

She cried out, as she had done in so many dreams before, 'Look! A whole floor of rooms I didn't know were there!' Her words echoed back to her down the narrow vault, and instead of the usual pleasure and triumph, she felt an extraordinary reluctance to look any further. A cold wind blew down and made her shiver, her teeth chattered. She woke, then, as usual, on the verge of discovery, but instead of regretting that she hadn't had time to find something wonderful, she felt more as if she had just escaped some danger.

'Laurie, you look terrible! You really must go to bed earlier,' her mother said, the next day.

'I'm all right, Mum. Don't fuss!'

'You've got a headache again. Haven't you?'

'Just a bit. I'll stop working earlier tonight,' Laurie promised. But though she'd have been grateful for the excuse not to lean her tired head over her books, she didn't want to go to bed. 'To sleep! Perchance to dream; ay, there's the rub,' she might have exclaimed with Hamlet. As soon as she lost consciousness at night, she was back at the foot of the wide stairs, or already in the gallery, under the gaze of the portraits, which seemed to stare at her with patient, long-dead eyes. She was always walking towards the small concealed door, unwilling, but unable to stop herself. On this particular night, she did hesitate in front of a picture she didn't remember noticing before. It was the portrait of a girl of about her own age, looking straight out at Laurie with tired, deeply shadowed eyes. She was very pale, and there was a rigidity about her expression and her attitude which made her appear tightly-strung, like the string of a bow, just about to snap. She might have been poised for flight, or to meet some danger. Her pale, lint-blonde hair was dragged back from her forehead so tightly that it made Laurie's own forehead ache. Without thinking, she put a hand up to her brow, and as she did so, the girl in the painting moved too. She also lifted her hand to those strained hair-roots. Laurie was looking not at a picture, but at a mirror. She was seeing her own reflection.

She ran from it. But she was running towards the little door and, under her hand, it sprang open. She saw the mean treads of the winding stair and, for the first time, she put one foot on the lowest step. But she was paralysed by fear of the horror that was beckoning to her from the region above. She cried out, 'What is it? What is it?' She heard a voice, which seemed to come from inside her own head, answer. 'It is the fatal floor. The fatal floor.'

She screamed then. She woke screaming, with both hands trying to contain her bursting head. She saw her mother's face, now close to hers, now distant, carried backwards and forwards by waves of pain. She couldn't count time, she didn't know what eternity passed before there was a doctor, a needle in her arm, unconsciousness.

Then brief moments of waking when she was being wrapped, carried, jolted; more needles bringing relief from screaming agony. Then at last a slow waking to pain of a different quality, dull, aching, bearable. She was in hospital. She had had major surgery on her brain. Someone had shaved off all her hair, she looked horrible. But she was recovering. She was sane.

Some time later, the surgeon came to approve. 'What was it?' Laurie asked.

'We took out a whopping great blood clot. It was taking up far too much room inside your head. No wonder you had headaches.'

'How'd the clot get there?'

'You had a genetic weakness of one of the blood vessels. That means you were born with it, it wasn't due to anything you did. These things sometimes run in families. Don't look so worried. It won't happen again.'

'How do you know it won't?'

'Because I did a very good job on you. Now you're all neat and tidy upstairs,' the surgeon said, and left to visit his next patient.

'Upstairs. A fatal floor. A fatal flaw,' Laurie said, trying the words out.

'What's that supposed to mean?' her mother asked.

'Nothing. Mum! Can I have a wig till my hair grows again? A proper one.'

'I'll see if I can get one or two for you to try,' her mother said.

'Get a black one. Or, I'll tell you what. Auburn. I've always wanted to be red.'

'I'll get one of every colour they've got. Only don't get excited. You ought to try to have a sleep now.'

Laurie shut her eyes. She seemed to spend a great deal of her time asleep, even short waking periods left her tired.

Now thoughts and images floated through her head. They began to interweave and to grow confused, while a part of her mind which was still awake was saying, 'I'm falling asleep. I'm falling . . .' Then she was standing in a rutted country lane. Through the thin stems of the trees she saw the front of the untidy, friendly cottage which belonged to her, and in her dream she cried out joyfully, 'I'm here again! I'm here!'

Real Characters

He met them, the extraordinary brother and sister, at the celebration party. For the first time in his life, Edward had won a literary prize. He had known beforehand, of course, that his book was one of the six short-listed, but the announcement of the winner had not been made until the assembled guests had drunk their pre-dinner drinks, had got through the three main courses of the grand dinner, and were leaning back in their chairs, mellowed by good food and wine. Then the Chairman stood up, made a short routine speech praising each of the six novels in extravagant terms, and finally read out their titles in reverse order of merit. Edward was amazed as the list grew shorter and his name had not yet been mentioned. Then he had to come to terms with the fact that he was the prize-winner. His book had been judged the best suspense novel of the year. He was not only to receive the modest cheque, he would also benefit, if he was lucky, from television or film rights as well.

Edward was surprised, but he did feel that the success was deserved. He had taken a great deal of trouble over this book. He had had to re-write large parts of it several times, making drastic changes to the details of the plot, and also to some of the characters. Maggie, the heroine, whose sudden disappearance during a visit to a picture gallery – probably the National or the Tate, he had not specified – formed the basis of the mystery, had remained much the same from his first conception to his final draft; her family, however, had altered considerably. Her husband, Jake, who had originally been an amiable, hardworking business man, degenerated into a power-crazy tycoon who regularly drank too much. Maggie's only brother, a country solicitor at first, became a junior Civil Servant with access to secret files, whose sudden death in the Adriatic while on holiday gave rise to speculation about his integrity. There had been leaks from his department. Had Alec been a secret agent, a spy? Had he died by accident? Could it have been suicide, or even murder? These additions had contributed to the complexity and interest of the main plot, and Edward had been pleased with them.

The most fundamental changes had taken place in Maggie's two children. These had once been nondescript teenage boys of no great importance in the story; but when Edward had finished with them, the older had turned into a heroin addict, a liar and a thief, totally untrustworthy in every way. The younger had undergone a sex change, and was now a seventeen-year-old daughter, wayward and rebellious and outstandingly beautiful. Edward had sweated blood over these changes, and he knew that they contributed to the credibility of the plot and to the depth of his characters. He felt that he had at last achieved what he had always wanted: to tell a story with plenty of mystery and suspense, which involved real characters, not merely the cardboard figures which appeared in so many works of the same kind.

After the presentation, and after Edward's short speech of modest gratitude, people left their tables and walked about, greeting old friends and rivals, acquaintances and enemies. Edward obligingly posed for the press photographers, holding a copy of his book in front of him like a shield, and feeling foolish. There were too many people in the large room, he was uncomfortably jostled by the crowd. He managed to make his way over to a corner, where he could at least lean against a wall, and there he remained, holding an untouched glass of brandy which had been thrust into his hand.

But he was mistaken if he thought that here he would not attract attention. Fellow novelists, publishers, people he knew well and people he didn't remember ever having seen before, were constantly passing and greeting him. 'Hi, Edward! Splendid!' That was Benjamin, one of the rival novelists, whose book had not even made the short list. 'Hullo! You and I must have a long talk, my boy.' That was Jack, his agent, who might well beam at him; Jack was going to get quite a share of the total profits, without having so far done a hand's turn for it. 'Eddie, darling! I hope it's a whacking big cheque' with a warm scented kiss from Maria, triumphant in yet another West End starring role, and the wife of one of his personal friends. Joe came up a moment later. 'Congratulations, Ed. Why don't you write a play for Maria next? I'll bet you could pull off something better than the trash she's in just now.'

He was just going to take his first sip of brandy, when he saw a couple approaching him who were complete strangers. The young man was unattractive: slouching, scowling, with tangled, unwashed hair and a three days' growth of beard. But the girl was stunning. She could be any age from eighteen to twenty-five; tall, bright brown hair, a wide forehead, very dark blue eyes, a lovely mouth. They were pushing through the crowds in a purposeful way, until they were standing directly in front of him, almost penning him in. Edward was sure he had never set eyes on either of them before, but a successful author must not shun his readers, so he waited politely for them to open the conversation.

The young man started by saying, in what sounded an almost hostile tone, 'Now we've got you! You can't get away.'

Edward agreed. 'No, I can't. Why should I want to?'

'Why should you want to? That's rich!' the young man said. His laugh was as unpleasant as his appearance, Edward thought. He looked at the beautiful girl.

'We've been looking for you,' she said.

Now Edward understood. Autograph hunters. There had been several during the evening, coming up shyly with requests that he would inscribe something for them in their copies of his book. He said, 'Got your copy there?' and felt in his pocket for his Parker pen.

'Keep your hands out of your pockets,' the young man said; it was a creditable imitation of an American gangster movie. Edward took his hand out of his pocket immediately, and attempted to laugh at what he thought was a very poor joke.

'So sorry. I thought you wanted me to write something . . .' he began.

'Want you to write? Us? Haven't you done enough harm already?' the young man said, pushing his face disagreeably close to Edward's. He smelt unwashed, and there was another curious odour which Edward couldn't identify.

'I'm afraid I don't understand,' he said, wishing he hadn't placed himself in this corner from which there was no retreat.

'Oh yes, you do. Look at me. Are you proud of what you've done to me?' the young man asked.

'To you? But I've never met you before! How can I

possibly have done anything to you?' Edward asked, completely mystified.

'Never met me! Never met your own creation? Never met your children? That's what we are, aren't we?' the young man persisted.

He's crazy. I've got landed with a madman, Edward thought. Aloud he said, 'You're making a mistake, you know. I haven't got any children, and if I had . . .'

'They wouldn't be like me, you were going to say. They might be like Imogen, though, mightn't they? Take a good look at her. Never seen her before either?'

'I don't . . .' Edward said, then hesitated. Imogen? The name seemed familiar, but he could have sworn he would never have forgotten a young goddess like this. She looked back at him, neutral, without a flicker of recognition in her eyes. The young man was speaking again. 'She's got you to thank for her looks. And for her rotten character. And for the fact that she's got a junkie for a brother and an alcoholic for her Dad. And you needn't think her looks are going to be anything but a problem for a girl like her. You've done for both of us. Why couldn't you leave us alone? We were all right before you came along with your grand ideas about creating "real characters". Real! Look at us! Are you pleased with what you've done?'

The girl spoke now. 'He did just one thing right. I never wanted to be a boy.'

Either they're mad, or I am, Edward thought. Or could he suddenly have become incapably drunk? But the brandy glass in his hand was nearly full and quite steady. A passer-by called out, 'Edward! Great news, you deserved it! Marge says come to supper on Sunday, haven't seen you for ages.'

Edward called back, 'Thanks, lovely,' without really knowing what he was saying. The young man was talking again. 'She makes a pretty girl, doesn't she? No one would guess she used to be a Martin. Like I was Mark. We weren't in trouble then. I was going to be a musician, remember? But that was before Dad started drinking and while Uncle Alec was still around. You murdered him!' he suddenly spat at Edward.

'That's absurd. I've never murdered anyone.'

'You killed Alec. First you smeared his character, then you drowned him.'

The accusation took Edward's breath away. He did not answer.

'Alec. Maggie's brother. And I'm Johnny, Maggie's son. This here's Imogen, who's got looks, but not a rag of self-respect left. All your own work. I hope you're proud of it.'

Edward stared at him. Characters from fiction do not suddenly come to confront their authors. This was not just a delusion, it was a nightmare.

'I'm going to kill you when we get out of here,' the young man said.

'He means it, you know,' the beautiful girl said.

'Tell him not to. It wasn't my . . . I didn't mean . . .' Edward said to the girl.

'Why should I? I've never seen anyone killed before,' the girl said, and Edward remembered, with a lurch of the heart, that he had deliberately made Imogen cold and ruthless, out for sensation at any cost.

'I'll report you! I'll get police protection!' Edward said to the young man.

'Protection against a character out of your own book? Who do you think will get put away for that?' the young man said.

Edward heard himself say, 'You can't! It's not . . . not fair!' like an echo of his nursery days. He said, desperately, 'I'll change it all. I'll write another book . . . a sequel. I'll make it all come right for you. I can't do more than that.'

'Is that a promise?' the young man asked.

'Yes! Of course it is. If only you'll leave me alone. After all, if you kill me now, I won't have a chance, will I?' It was a desperate, insane cunning.

'I might just give you the chance. What about it, Ginny?' the young man asked the beautiful girl. She shrugged her shoulders. 'Makes no difference to me. If you believe him . . .'

'I swear I'll do it,' Edward pleaded.

The young man drew back a little, as if to let Edward pass him and escape. 'Perhaps I'll let you go now. Let you go home and start on this great new work. Just for a time. But I'm not going to lose sight of you. Wherever you are, I'll be somewhere not far off. Ready for you. You know that?'

'He'll never feel safe,' the beautiful girl gloated.

'But you'll give me time. It wouldn't do you any good to kill me right away,' Edward said, edging his way past the brother and sister towards the safety of the still crowded room.

'I'll give you time.'

'Is that a promise?' Edward was beyond the couple now, escaping, he hoped back to sanity. But the young man's voice followed him. 'A promise? Don't you remember what you made me? I'm a liar. You shouldn't believe a word I say.'

Bill's Ghost

'So just as you're going to sleep, you hear this noise,' Bill said.

'What noise?'

'Clank, clank. Clank, clank, clank.'

'Horrible noise. What is it?' Emily asked rapturously.

'Rusty chains.'

'What's rusty chains for?'

'Rusty chains is what ghosts drag around with them.'

'What's ghosts?' Emily asked.

'People who come back after they're dead and buried,' Bill said.

Emily considered this. 'What they come for?'

'They come at night and walk round your bed and groan. Like this.' Bill produced a groan that started low and ended with a high-pitched wail. He found it fairly frightening himself, but Emily was delighted with it and immediately tried to imitate it.

'I'm a ghost!' she said.

'You can't be. You're not dead. Anyway, you're much too fat to be a ghost. Ghosts are thin. And you can see right through them,' Bill said.

'Like my fish?'

'No!' Bill shouted, exasperated.

'I can see through my fish. Sometimes. A bit.'

'That's because of the kind of fish he is. You can't ever see through a person, not unless he's a ghost.'

'Doesn't he wear any clothes? That's rude,' Emily said.

'He wears armour. Like in the picture in the sitting-room. To fight in, so he doesn't get hurt. His armour clanks too.'

'Clank, clank,' Emily said, with gusto.

Bill felt that she was treating the subject too lightly. Ghosts were not meant to be enjoyed. He said, 'He's had his head cut off.'

'Is there blood?' Emily asked.

'Lots of blood. Dripping all over the place.'

Emily sighed with pleasure.

'Where's his poor head, then?'

'Under his arm,' Bill said.

'I can put my head under my arm,' Emily said.

'Not like that, silly. With his arm at his side. Like this.'

'I could do that too,' Emily said.

'Not like he can. Because his head is cut off at the neck, see? So he can carry it like . . . like a football.'

'Does it hurt?'

'It did when he had it cut off. You just think what it would be like if someone came along with a sword and chopped your head off.'

'Poor head,' Emily said.

'You'd scream.'

'Wouldn't scream.'

'Who wouldn't scream?' Bill's mother asked as she came into the room.

'Wouldn't if someone cut my head off,' Emily said.

'What on earth have you been talking about?'

Bill said in a hurry, 'About knights in armour, fighting.' But he wasn't quick enough. His mother heard Emily say, 'Poor ghosts you can see through like my fish.'

42

'Bill! I've told you before, you're not to frighten Emily by telling her horrible stories just before she goes to bed.'

'Horrible stories,' Emily gloated.

'What did you say to her?' Bill's mother demanded.

'Blood dripping. Carries his head like a football,' Emily said.

'Now, Emily! You're not to take any notice of what Bill was saying. All sensible people know there aren't any such things as ghosts,' her mother said.

'No ghosts?' Emily asked.

'No, darling. No nasty ghosts.'

Emily burst into tears.

'There! See what you've done! You've frightened her badly. It's all right, Emily, pet. Bill was just making it all up.'

But Emily wouldn't be comforted. She was taken away by her mother to be bathed and fed with hot cocoa and sponge fingers before she was put to bed. Bill was left with the disagreeable promise that his Mum would have something to say to him later. What made it all the more annoying was that he knew that what Emily was crying for was the abrupt end to the idea of ghosts with rusty chains and dripping necks. To be put back firmly into an ordinary world where only fish could be seen through and no one carried his head like a football under his arm, was too disappointing. Bill couldn't think why his Mum was so anxious that he shouldn't frighten Emily. He'd never been able to do it yet.

Bill went to bed that night feeling sore. His Mum had told him off, his Dad had taken up the story and solemnly warned him against repeating the offence. He skipped his washing, in a don't-care mood, and went to bed at odds with the world. He wasn't supposed to read in bed in case he woke Emily, who shared his room. He lay gloomily in bed, thinking up tortures suitable for inconvenient younger sisters, until at last he fell, rather miserably, asleep.

He was woken by a noise he didn't recognize. Not the swish of the passing cars in the road outside. Not footsteps. Not the creak of the door, which meant that his Mum was glancing in. Not the gentle scratching of Mrs Twitchett, the cat, asking for a warm bit of a bed. Not the sound of rain on the roof. A noise like . . .

Clank. Clank. Clank.

'Who is it?' Bill asked. No one answered, but the something went Clank again, and there was a grating, metallic sound; it could have been the rattle of rusty chains being dragged along the ground.

Then there was a silence. It was complete, except for the hammering of Bill's heart, like waves pounding a shore; through it he could hear the tiny tick of his bedside clock. He could feel his hair standing up on his head. He was extremely frightened. However, he did not scream.

The room remained quite black and quiet.

Bill stretched out his hand to the table by his bed. His fingers closed over the torch he always had there. Almost the bravest thing he had ever done in his life was when he pressed the switch and shone the beam towards the place where those mysterious sounds had come from.

The batteries were old and it was a feeble ray of light. It was reflected back dimly from the unpolished armour of the breastplate and the plates covering the upper arms. Not from a helmet. Because above the shoulders the figure strangely ended with a very short neck. The head which should have topped the neck was being carried comfortably under the person's left arm. It was a good-looking head, with dark curly hair, a long nose, enquiring eyes and a mouth curved in a distinctly friendly smile.

'Hi!' said the mouth.

Bill wasn't ready to answer this. The beam from the torch wavered slightly. Bill sat and gazed.

'Aren't you pleased to see me?' the mouth asked.

'I'm . . . Who are you?' Bill asked. He now noticed something else, very peculiar. Through the dim armour, through the agreeably conversing head, he distinctly saw the familiar furniture and walls of his bedroom.

'You said to come, so I came. That's right, isn't it?' the mouth said, reproachfully.

'But . . .'

'I'm exactly like you said,' the ghost said.

'But . . .'

'You can't say you weren't expecting me,' the ghost said. He sounded disappointed, and Bill felt bad. But he couldn't get used to carrying on a conversation with a head worn so very much below the shoulders. He said, 'Isn't it. . . . Is it . . . uncomfortable having your head under your arm like that?'

'Agony,' said the ghost, very cheerful indeed.

There was a short pause.

'Does it feel peculiar. . . ? I mean does it feel funny to be . . . well, to be so that I can see right through you?' Bill asked.

The ghost was surprised. 'Of course not. I'd have thought it would feel funny knowing that people can't see what's behind you. You must keep out an awful lot of light,' the ghost said.

It was a new idea to Bill. He said, 'I suppose I'm used to it.'

'Exactly. That's how I feel. I'm used to being the way I am,' the ghost said. Another short pause.

'Oh! Sorry! I was forgetting,' the ghost said suddenly. The mouth under the arm opened wide and groaned. It was a tremendous sound.

'Sh . . . ssssssh!'

'You wanted a groan,' the ghost said, hurt.

'Yes, but. . . . You might wake Emily.'

'Is that Emily?' the ghost asked. The eyes in the head under the arm rolled towards the hump in Emily's bed.

'Yes. She's asleep. But if she wakes up and sees you, she'll scream.'

The ghost moved over to look at Emily, clanking softly as he went.

'She's wearing her head on top too,' he said, disappointed.

'Of course she is.'

'I'd just hoped that one of you might look a bit more ordinary.'

'Ordinary?'

'Like I am. With a see-through body and a head you can put anywhere you happen to want it, instead of having it always stuck in one place. It must be very boring.'

'It isn't boring. You can always turn it round if you want to see something.'

'Like this?' The ghost gave his detached head a spin, and it whirled like a top under his arm, eyes rolling. It made Bill feel dizzy to look at it.

'Not a bit like that,' he said.

The head stopped spinning. 'You'll be telling me next that you can't come and go as you please,' the ghost said.

'What do you mean? Of course I can come and go.'

'Like this?' the ghost asked. And disappeared.

Bill drew a breath of relief. But the relief didn't last. 'Like this?' the ghost's voice said again. Bill turned his head—safely anchored on his neck—and saw the ghost standing on the further side of Emily's bed.

'You can do that?' the ghost asked.

'Not quite like that. I just walk. Or run.'

'Not quick enough,' the ghost said.

'Not quick enough for what?' Bill asked.

'Well. Suppose we were talking, like we are now. And suppose the sun rose. I'd have to disappear. Double quick.'

'Would you?' Bill asked hopefully.

'Don't worry. I reckon we've got another four hours yet. Or suppose someone else came into this room. I'd have to disappear then too. At once. No time to run. How could you manage that?'

Bill left this question unanswered. He said, 'Why would you have to disappear if someone else came into the room?'

'My helmet, you are ignorant! Don't you really know that? I'm here because you believe in me. If someone came in who didn't believe in me, I'd have to go. See?'

Bill didn't entirely see. What he did understand, however, was that there might be a chance of dismissing the ghost before the sun rose. He couldn't stand another four hours of this, that was certain.

'You'd have to go and you wouldn't come back again?' he asked.

'Not unless I was sent for, like you sent for me this evening,' the ghost said.

'It was very good of you to come,' Bill said politely.

'It was a pleasure. And now you know how to get in touch with me, I expect we'll be seeing a lot of each other. You can explain to me your peculiar way of living. What it's like to be so slow and so solid. I can't remember, it's such a long time since I was like that,' the ghost said.

'Would you do something for me?' Bill asked.

'Anything,' the ghost said warmly.

'I wish you'd groan again.'

'You stopped me! You said to shush. Suppose I wake her?' The ghost's eyes turned to Emily again.

'I've just thought. She'd love to hear you,' Bill said.

'Then certainly.' The ghost re-arranged his head and the mouth opened wide. The groan was blood-curdling. Bill felt a cold shiver run down his spine.

'How was that?' the ghost asked.

'Great! Please do it again.'

The ghost gave another tremendous groan. Emily's sleeping form stirred.

'Enough?' the ghost suggested.

'Just one more,' Bill pleaded.

The third groan was a magnificent performance. It was deeper and longer and louder than anything Bill could have produced. It was accompanied by the clank of rusty chains. If they hadn't just been having such a sane, if unusual, conversation, Bill could have believed that this was one of those historical ghosts, come to terrify and to bring bad news. He found the groan fairly frightening in spite of the friendliness of this agreeable ghost. He shut his eyes and hoped.

As the groan died away, there was a rustle from Emily's bed. The hump drew itself together, flattened out and rolled over. Emily's pink face rose over the bedclothes, eyes blinking, mouth open with surprise at what she saw.

She saw Bill, sitting up in bed, eyes shut, his torch in his hand. The beam was faint and flickering. It lit up the middle of her bed, a slanting patch of wall beyond, a chair with her clothes on it. It lit up nothing else.

She said, 'You woke me!'

Bill's eyes flew open. He looked first at the other side of her bed. He said, 'Emily?'

'What you looking at?'

Bill said, 'Nothing. You can see, there's nothing there.'

'Nothing there,' Emily said.

'No. There isn't, is there?'

48

Emily wasn't interested in discussing nothing. She said, 'You made a horrible noise.'

'I didn't mean to,' Bill said, not quite truthfully.

'You groaned.'

'I'm not going to any more. Lie down and go to sleep again.'

'You going to sleep?' Emily asked.

Bill said, 'Yes,' and switched off his torch to show that he meant it. He lay down. He heard Emily pull the bedclothes up as she lay down too.

'Dark,' said Emily.

Bill hoped his sister was falling asleep in the silence that followed. But suddenly a voice said, 'Can't go to sleep.'

'Shut your eyes.'

'Tell me a story,' Emily's voice said.

'No.'

'Tell me about ghost.'

'NO!'

'Poor ghost.'

'Go to sleep, Emily.'

'Wish ghost was real and would make clank, clank.'

'Emily!'

'Tomorrow. Tell . . . about . . . ghost . . . blood . . . clank. . . .' Emily's voice died out as sleep overcame her. Bill stayed awake for at least another five minutes, during which he made a firm resolution. Tell Emily, or anyone, about ghosts another time? As if he hadn't learned his lesson? Not if he knew it. Not ever again.

Crossing Over

If she hadn't been fond of dogs, she would never have volunteered for this particular job. When her class at school were asked if they would give up some of their spare time towards helping old people, most of the tasks on offer had sounded dreary. Visiting housebound old men and women, making them cups of tea and talking to them; she hadn't fancied that, and she wasn't any good at making conversation, let alone being able to shout loud enough for a deaf person to hear. Her voice was naturally quiet. She didn't like the idea of doing anyone else's shopping, she wasn't good enough at checking that she'd got the right change. The check-out girls in the supermarket were too quick, ringing up the different items on the cash register. Nor did she want to push a wheelchair to the park. But walking old Mrs Matthews' dog, that had seemed like something she might even enjoy. She couldn't go every evening, but she would take him for a good long run on the Common on Saturdays, and on fine evenings, when the days were longer, she'd try to call for him after school some weekdays. She had started out full of enthusiasm.

What she hadn't reckoned with was the dog himself. Togo was huge, half Alsatian, half something else which had given him long woolly hair, permanently matted and dirty. Once, right at the beginning, she had offered to bathe and groom him, but Mrs Matthews had been outraged by the suggestion, was sure the poor creature would catch cold, and at the sight of the comb, Togo backed and growled and showed his teeth. It was as much as she could do to fasten and unfasten his leash, and he did not make that easy. The early evening walks weren't quite so bad, because there wasn't time to take him to the Common, so he stayed on the leash all the time. Even then he was difficult to manage. He seemed to have had no training and he certainly had no manners. He never stopped when she told him to, never came when she called him, so that every Saturday, when she dutifully let him run free among the gorse bushes and little trees on the Common, she was afraid she might have to return to Mrs Matthews without the dog, confessing that he had run away. Mrs Matthews did not admit that Togo was unruly and difficult to manage, any more than she would admit that he smelled. It was only a feeling that she shouldn't go back on her promise to perform this small service to the community that kept the girl still at the disagreeable task.

This particular evening was horrible. She'd been kept later at school than usual, and although it was already March, the sky was overcast, it was beginning to get dark, and a fine drizzling rain made the pavements slippery. Togo was in a worse mood than usual. He had slouched along, stopping for whole minutes at lampposts and dustbins and misbehaving extravagantly in the most inconvenient places, in spite of her frantic tugs at the leash to try to get him off the pavement. He was too strong for her to control, and he knew it. She almost believed that he had a spite against her, and enjoyed showing that he didn't have to do anything she wanted, as if it wasn't bad enough having to go out in public with an animal so unkempt and anti-social.

They reached the zebra crossing on the hill. The traffic was moving fast, as it always did during the evening rush-hour. She would have to wait for a break before she could step off the pavement, especially as, in the half dark, she knew from her Dad's comments when he was driving, pedestrians on the road were not easy to see. She stood still and dragged at Togo's lead. But Togo did not mean to be dictated to by a little schoolgirl, and after a moment's hesitation, he pulled too. He was off, into the middle of the on-coming traffic, wrenching at the leash, which she had twisted round her hand in order to get a better grip. She threw all her weight against his, but she was no match for him. She thought she felt the worn leather snap, she heard the sound of screaming brakes and someone shouted. She had time to think, 'What am I going to say to Mrs Matthews?', before her head swam and she thought she was going to faint.

She found herself standing on the further side of the road. She saw a huddle of people, surrounding stationary cars. Two drivers had left their vehicles and were abusing each other. As the crowd swayed, she saw the bonnet of a red car crumpled by its contact with the back of a large yellow van. She saw, too, a dark stain on the road surface. Blood. Blood made her feel sick, and her head swam again. She hesitated, knowing that she ought to go among the watching people to make herself look, perhaps to try to explain how Togo had pulled, how she hadn't been strong enough to hold him back. Someone should be told whose dog he was. Someone would have to go and break the terrible news to Mrs Matthews.

As she was considering this, she heard the siren of a police car and the two-note call of an ambulance. She thought, 'Perhaps someone got badly hurt in one of the cars, and it's all my fault.' Her courage evaporated, and she turned away from the accident and began to walk, on legs that trembled, up the hill towards her own home. She thought, 'I'll go and tell Mum.' But then she remembered how much Mrs Matthews loved horrible Togo, how she talked about him as her only friend, and how dreadful it was going to be for her to open her front door to find a policeman telling her that her dog was dead. Besides, the policeman might say that it was all her, the girl's, fault. She had to go first to Mrs Matthews' house, to break the news gently, and also to explain that she had tried her best to prevent the accident.

She found that she must have been walking really fast, which was surprising, considering how much she was dreading the ordeal in front of her. She had reached the grocer's and the newspaper shop at the top of the High Street almost before she'd realized. She saw Sybil Grainger coming out of the newspaper shop, and she was ready to say, 'Hi!' and to pretend that there was nothing wrong, but luckily Sybil seemed not to have seen her. She turned the corner into Grange Road, relieved that she hadn't had to carry on a conversation. Grange Road also seemed shorter than usual; now she had to go along Fenton Crescent till she reached the small side street where Mrs Matthews lived, in one of the row of little old cottages known as Paradise Row.

Her heart beat furiously as she unlatched the small wooden gate and walked the short distance up to the front door, rehearsing exactly how to say what she had to. She lifted the knocker. As it came down on the wood, it made a hollow, echoing sound.

Extraordinary. From the other side of the door, she heard something very much like Togo's deep, menacing growl. She must be in such a state of nerves that she was imagining impossible things. Or perhaps when she felt faint out there in the road, she had fallen and hit her head and been concussed. She felt her scalp, under the straight, silky hair, but she couldn't find any tender spots. She waited. Mrs Matthews was arthritic and always took a long time to answer the door, and there was no hurry for the message she was going to receive.

Steps came slowly, dragging a little, along the passage. The door opened, and she braced herself for the shock she was about to administer and the scolding she was certainly going to receive.

But when Mrs Matthews looked out, she behaved in a very peculiar way. Instead of saying immediately, 'Where's Togo?' she asked nothing of her visitor, but bent forward and peered out, looking up and down the short row of cottages, as if she were searching for something or someone who might be coming or going in the street. Her head with its thinning grey hair was so close that the girl stepped back, opening her mouth to begin her explanation. But what she saw in the passage behind the old woman stopped her from uttering a sound.

At the further end of the passage was a dog. Togo. Togo, whole, apparently unharmed, his collar round his neck, and the end of the broken leash still attached, dragging behind him.

For a moment she thought he was going to spring forward and attack her. Then she saw that, instead, he was backing, shrinking as far away as he could get. He was making a curious noise, not a howl, nor a growl, but a sort of whine. She noticed that he was trembling. She had never seen Togo tremble before. He was showing whites round his yellow eyes and the short hair round his muzzle was bristling.

She started to speak. But Mrs Matthews appeared not to have heard her. She was turning back to calm the terrified dog. She was saying, 'Whatever's the matter with you, Togo? Think you're seeing a ghost?'

Meeting Eric

'We haven't flitted about from place to place like this since
we were students,' Sylvia said, when Peter suggested that
they should cut short their stay in Rotterdam and go on to
Vienna a day early.

'Well? Now we've both retired, we don't need to feel
tied to anything. Not even our own plans,' Peter said.

'D'you remember when the kids were little and we
thought we were lucky if we got a week off by ourselves
twice a year?'

'I'll never forget that time we spent the week with Eric
and Nancy, sharing a cottage in the Lakes. Never stopped
raining for an hour. That was a fine week's holiday.'

'Peter! Has Eric got a list of all the places we might be
going to? Nancy's keen on getting him to go away this
summer, and she thinks he just might if they could meet up
with us somewhere. She says he's been working too hard
and she's a bit worried. He's been losing weight, and she's
sure it's overwork.'

'I told him about Vienna, but I don't think he'd want to
go to a city, he's more of an outdoor holiday-maker. He
knows about Nîmes, and Athens, of course. If he comes to
meet us at all, I reckon it's likely to be in Greece.'

Vienna was sparkling and hot and crowded. Peter and
Sylvia wandered round, seeing the sights. A friend of

Peter's managed to get them tickets for the opera, and the night before they were to leave, they found themselves sitting in a tiny box in the second circle, so much to the side that they faced, not the stage, but other boxes directly opposite. In the intervals between the acts of the opera, which was long and beautiful and tragic, Peter and Sylvia and their hosts wandered about the huge Opera House, drinking cold white wine and, in the case of the hosts, greeting friends. They were back in the little box just before the last act, when Peter, sitting in front, leaned forward and waved.

'You have seen a friend?' the Herr Doktor asked.

'One of my oldest friends. There, in the box opposite. Look, Sylvia! It's Eric!'

'I can't see that far,' Sylvia said.

'Please! Take my *Operngucker* — my opera glass — to look,' the Herr Doktor said. But as Sylvia raised the glasses to her eyes, the lights dimmed and the orchestra began to play. It was impossible to speak or to move. It wasn't until the applause at the end of the opera that Peter was able to say, 'He'll probably come round to the box to catch us.'

But Eric didn't. There was a frightening crush as the audience crowded out of the Opera House, and Peter and Sylvia then discovered, rather to their dismay, that they were being taken by their host to a late supper in one of Vienna's famous restaurants. It was the early hours of the next morning before they were back in their hotel. But there was no message from Eric. 'He's probably forgotten that we're leaving at crack of dawn tomorrow,' Peter said, climbing wearily into bed.

'It isn't even tomorrow. It's today.'

'So much the worse. I shall try to sleep on the plane.'

'Perhaps he's going to meet us in Paris, then we'll fly on

together to Nîmes,' Sylvia suggested. Peter was already asleep. His only answer to this was a light snore.

But there were no messages from Eric at the Paris airport. They flew to Nîmes that evening and were delighted to find it much emptier than Vienna; but there were still no signs of Eric and Nancy. They hired a car and drove out into the hilly, warm countryside around. Every evening when they returned to their hotel, they expected to find that Eric had called; every evening they were disappointed. Finally, they decided to go off for a couple of nights a little further afield. The next day, they drove through the Camargue to the small walled town of Aigues Mortes, where once a King Louis of France set sail on a Crusade for the Holy Land. Since those days, the sea has retreated, leaving the town on the edge of an expanse of marsh; but it is still a beautiful town, so small that you can walk round the encircling battlements in something like half an hour.

It was a broiling day, and Peter, though he wouldn't admit it, was tired by the time they had climbed up to the wall walk and had gone nearly half-way round. 'We don't have to do the whole thing. Let's go down and go back through the town,' Sylvia said, noticing his fatigue.

'Nonsense! It's much better up here.'

'Sure you feel up to going round the rest of the way?'

'Of course. Don't fuss!'

'It's just . . . You said you had a sort of pain last night.'

'Indigestion. Come on!' Peter said, then suddenly stopped and pointed. 'Look! Down there! Quick, he's just going round that corner.'

'Who? What?' Sylvia asked.

'Eric, of course. There! No, he's gone.'

'Eric? Are you sure? He didn't know we were going to be here.'

'You seem to think that Eric only goes where he's going to find us. This is a well-known curiosity ... sight ... whatever you like to call it. Of course, if he's in Nîmes, he'd come here. Just as we did.'

'Did he see you, d'you think?'

'I think so. He'll probably be waiting for us the further side of the battlements. Let's get there quickly to find him.'

But Eric was not waiting for them when they came down from the wall. Nor was he in the car park, as Peter confidently expected.

'Peter, are you quite sure it was Eric? You know how almost all very tall thin men, going a bit bald on top, can look the same in the distance.'

'I'm positive. Let's go straight back to Nîmes. He'll be at the hotel.'

'I thought we were going to stay tonight in Arles?'

'I'd rather give Arles a miss. I am a bit tired. I could do with a long cold drink and then going out with Eric and Nancy to some glamorous restaurant this evening.'

But Peter's plan could not be carried out. At the hotel in Nîmes, the receptionist was certain; there had been no messages, no one had called and asked for Peter and Sylvia. They had the long cool drink by themselves and, in view of Peter's indigestion of the night before, skipped the glamorous restaurant. They spent the next day quietly, not going far afield, but again Eric failed to turn up. 'Never mind. He's sure to meet us in Greece,' Peter consoled Sylvia, and himself.

Nîmes had been warm. Athens was hot, and busy, and dusty, and demanding. And Eric was not at their hotel to greet them. After waiting in all one morning, in vain, for a call, Peter agreed that before they flew on to Crete, they must visit the Acropolis, which he had seen years before, but which Sylvia did not know. They joined a conducted tour, and for two long, hot hours trailed round behind the English-speaking guide, drinking in Culture. Finally, when the visit was to end with a tour of the museum, Sylvia took pity on Peter's tired boredom, and suggested that he should stay and rest somewhere, while she dutifully followed the rest of the party. She left Peter sitting outside the little temple on the north of the Acropolis. He preferred to face the huge bronze door, out of sight of those long-suffering maidens who act as pillars and hold up the heavy roof on their heads.

When she came back half an hour later, the heat was beginning to give way to a comfortable warmth. As they walked slowly down the wide marble steps towards the road, Peter said, 'You might be right about my seeing Eric every time a tall thin chap comes into view. I could have sworn just now that he came through that door up there, but when I called out to him, he just shook his head and went away again.'

'Through which door?' Sylvia asked.

'The big doorway where the bronze door is that you admire so much.'

'But . . . Surely that door isn't ever opened?'

'Perhaps I dreamed it. I think I did nod off for a moment,' Peter said.

Sylvia wasn't quite satisfied with this explanation. She was glad that they were going on next day to Crete, where they could take life more easily. And Peter seemed less tired once they had settled into their hotel in Heraklion, and was as eager as she was to visit the bazaar, the museum, the little Venetian fort in the harbour and, of course, the site of Knossos, the city where King Minos had ruled over the island and where he kept the shameful secret, the bull-headed Minotaur, concealed in the labyrinth below his palace. 'Let's take the local bus and spend the whole day there. Then we won't have to hurry ourselves,' Peter suggested.

'Good idea. There's sure to be a place where we can get some sort of meal,' Sylvia agreed, thinking that out in the ruined palace, surrounded by stony fields and hills, Peter wouldn't be expecting Eric to turn up at any moment. To set her own mind at rest, however, she put through a long-distance call to Eric's home. It would be a relief to be able to tell Peter either that Eric was indeed on his way to meet them, or that he and Nancy had decided not to go away. But in fact there was nothing to tell Peter. When she had at last got through, the interference on the line was infuriatingly loud, and she could only just make out that the woman who answered was not Nancy, who was apparently unavailable for some inaudible reason. When she asked instead for Eric, there was an explosion of crackles and all Sylvia could understand was, she could not speak to him either. She decided not to relay this unsatisfactory lack of news to Peter, since it might only make him worry the more.

She was worried herself. She wished she'd been able to make out at least whether Eric and Nancy were still in England or not. After she and Peter had wandered around the ruins and reconstructions of the city for some time, he announced his intention of climbing the hill behind them so that he could look down and see the general lay-out from a height.

'I'll wait for you here,' Sylvia said.

'I won't be long. Then we'll go and look for some food. I could do with a salad and some red wine,' Peter said as he left her.

'Don't go too far. I don't want you overtired again.'

'I won't go further than that hump up there with the stones,' Peter said, and left Sylvia sitting on a fallen length of masonry, admiring a huge stone jar, large enough to hold at least two of Ali Baba's forty thieves.

He climbed slowly. The ground was rough and uneven, and he was soon short of breath, so that when he looked above him towards the hump, and joyfully recognized the figure standing there, he could not call out, as he meant to. All he could produce was a sort of croak. 'Eric! Thought you'd never catch up with us. When did you get here?'

There was no mistake this time, it really was Eric. He answered, 'Just now.'

'This morning? I didn't know ... You flew in?'

'You could say so,' Eric said.

'Where have you left Nancy? I hope she's here too.'

'Nancy's at home.'

'That's a shame! Nothing wrong, I hope?'

'Didn't you get her cable? In Rotterdam? I know she sent it to your hotel there.'

'Must have come after we'd gone. I didn't leave a forwarding address, because we weren't expecting to see you there. What happened? She isn't ill?'

'No, she's not ill. She'll be all right. She's a brave woman ...' Eric was saying, but Peter interrupted him.

'Was the cable saying you were coming to Vienna? I thought I saw you there. In the Opera House, unlikely as it seems.'

'Yes, I was there. I couldn't catch you in the crush afterwards.'

'Were you in Aigues Mortes too?'

'That's right. I only just missed you that time. But I almost got to you on the Acropolis.'

'Why didn't you come up and talk to me there?' Peter asked.

'I nearly did. Then I thought it'd be too hard on Sylvia, having to get you down in all those crowds.'

'Why should Sylvia have had to get me down? I'm perfectly capable of getting down myself.'

'You don't seem to understand. Oh! Of course. You never got Nancy's cable.'

'But that was a fortnight ago. Nearly.'

'That's right.'

'What was it about? What did Nancy say?'

'It was to tell you that I'd been taken into hospital. Emergency operation . . .'

'Eric, I am sorry! But you look fine now. How come they let you out so quickly?'

'They hadn't any choice. You could say I escaped, I suppose. Anyway, here I am. Come to fetch you.'

'Fetch me where to?' Peter asked. But Eric's only answer was to lean forward and to touch him lightly on the chest. An excruciating pain stabbed his breastbone and shot up to his shoulder. He heard Eric's voice. 'That's all. Now I'll show you the way.'

Sylvia, looking up, saw Peter reach the hump with the outcrop of stone. She saw him stop there, but he did not turn round to look down on Knossos, nor to wave to her. He seemed to hesitate. Then he threw out his hands and fell. Sylvia leapt to her feet and started towards him. She saw no one else on the hillside.

Where's Mervyn?

'You'll like the country. There'll be lambs and primroses and trees to climb. It's beautiful. Well, it will be, when the spring comes,' Celia's mother said.

Celia nodded. But she did not look at all certain that she would really like the country cottage which was going to be their home from now on. She was accustomed to the London flat where she had lived all her life. Her occupations, her school and her friends were all here.

'It's a dear little cottage. Just right for two of us,' her Mum said.

Celia still did not speak.

'You'll go to the school in the village, and I'm going to teach at the big school in the town. It's only a fifteen-minute ride in the school bus. When you're old enough you'll be coming there too.'

'I don't want to go to the country,' Celia said.

'I know, darling. But we can't stay here. The flat is too big for us now. And I've got to earn some money for us to live on. I was lucky to get this job at Withersham. And we were lucky to get the little cottage. I think you'll like it when we've settled in and you've found some friends.'

Celia's mother spoke more hopefully than she felt. Celia didn't make friends quickly. She had no brothers or sisters. She had always been a silent, solitary child, living much of her waking life in the removed, insulated world of the partially hearing. Celia was deaf. She had been deaf from birth. She had a hearing aid which helped her a lot, and her lip-reading was excellent. People who met Celia for the first time in quiet surroundings often did not realize just how far her hearing was impaired. But in the large echoing class-room, or out in the playground, reverberating with the shouts of a hundred lively children, Celia was often at a loss to hear or to make herself understood. It took time for other children to appreciate how quickly she could respond if they would take a little trouble. It was hard on Celia to have to start in a new school now, at the age of ten. Her mother worried about her.

They moved house on a cold, wet, windy day in March. It was a tiny cottage, and they hadn't been able to bring all their furniture or many possessions with them. Even so, they were still working, unpacking and putting away books on the new shelves, crockery into old cupboards, and clothes into chests, at eight o'clock that evening. Celia's mother was too tired to cook. 'We'll have to open a tin,' she said. So she was grateful, as well as surprised, when their new neighbour, old Mrs Treadgold, came to invite them into her next-door cottage that evening for supper. 'No trouble. She'd just made a meat pie, much too large for one.'

She had lived in the same cottage, number 44, she told them, all her life. Been born in the bedroom upstairs seventy-five years ago, had lived here when she married, had her own children here and had nursed her husband here in his last illness. She was friendly, comfortable, cheerful. She seemed to know by instinct just how to speak to Celia clearly and not too fast, so that Celia was never left out of the conversation. By the end of the evening, Celia and her mother went back to End Cottage warmed by more than Mrs Treadgold's hot pie and cocoa.

Where's Mervyn?

The school term began ten days later. Celia's mother could hardly spare a thought for what she might find in her own new class. She was wondering how Celia was going to manage in the Primary School in the village, whether the children would be patient and kind. She wished that she herself wasn't going to be out of the house – out of the village, in fact – all day. That meant that if things went wrong, Celia wouldn't be able to reach her until the end of the school afternoon. She knew that Celia was nervous too; but with her usual silent stoicism, Celia did not speak of what she was feeling. She ate less than usual, and if her mother asked if she was all right, she only nodded. On the morning of her first day at the new school, she set off, saying goodbye with a tight, pale smile that hurt.

She had the same smile for the rest of that week. Her mother ached for what she knew Celia must be enduring. But in answer to her questions, Celia said only, 'It's all right.' The other children, she said, were 'all right'. The work was 'all right'. She never asked if she might stay away from school. But then she knew that her mother couldn't also stay away from her job, and, as Celia's father had often said, Celia was a fighter. She would stick at something that had to be done, she hated to give up and admit defeat. All this was true, but it was hard for her mother to watch the silent struggle without being able to do much to help.

One day the following week, on her afternoon off, Celia's mother went to the village school for an interview with the headmistress. She wanted to ask about Celia's progress. The headmistress was encouraging, if not enthusiastic. Celia was doing quite well. She was a clever child, her written work was well above average. 'Was she making friends?' 'Difficult to tell, so early in the term. And, as you probably know, Mrs Temple, children aren't very quick to take to a child who is in any way . . . different. I don't mean that Celia isn't a very nice little girl, but her disability does rather . . . well . . . rather put her apart. Just at first. I'm sure that she'll settle in happily with us before very long. It's early days yet.'

Celia's mother remembered how endless even one day of unhappiness or anxiety could seem to a child of ten. It would be worse for a child without friends. She felt as if Celia were living through months of loneliness and despair.

It was in the third week of term that she noticed the change. Celia was leaving for school in the morning without that look of braced endurance. When her mother boarded the bus for her own job, Celia went off without a backward look. That week she was eating better, too. She did her homework without reminder. At their evening meal, she was as near chattering as she ever had been. When her mother asked, 'How are you getting on at school these days?' Celia said, as usual, 'All right.' But now she sounded as if she meant it, and though she didn't elaborate on the statement, her mother was reassured.

It was a day or two more before her mother asked any direct questions. At last, at the end of the week, she said, as casually as she could, 'Have you made any special friends at school yet?'

Celia looked at her before answering. But this was something she often did when she wasn't quite sure she had heard, or read the speaker's lips, correctly. Then she said, 'Yes.'

'Good! Who is she?'

'It isn't . . . He's a boy. Mervyn.'

'In your class?'

'I don't know.'

Her mother was surprised. The classes in the village

school were small. It was difficult to understand how Celia couldn't know exactly who was in her class and who wasn't.

'How old is he?'

'Ten. Same as me.'

'What's his other name? Mervyn what?'

'Don't know.'

That was all, at the time. Celia's mother thought about Celia's new friend a great deal. She wondered how the friendship had begun. She hadn't expected that it would be a boy who would be Celia's first friend here. Most boys of that age, she thought, were too anxious to belong to gangs of their own sex to bother with a girl, especially a girl with a hearing problem. But it was obvious that Celia was a great deal happier and was enjoying her days at school, and that was the really important thing.

Ten or twelve days later, when they were in the village grocery shop in the early evening, they were hailed by Janey Preston, Celia's young, pretty teacher. 'Hi, Mrs Temple! Hi, Celia! Hasn't it been a lovely day?'

It was a promise-of-spring day. Cool, fresh, but without the bite of the east wind which had tormented the April flowers and persisted well into May. Celia's mother agreed, they could begin to feel that spring, though late, was really nearly here. Janey was emphasizing how well Celia was doing in class. 'She's settled down with us really well,' she said, and Celia's mother noticed with gratitude that Janey spoke to Celia as well as to her mother, talking slowly and taking care to face Celia, so that what she couldn't hear, she could read, and she wouldn't feel left out. Presently Celia wandered over to look at a stack of confectionery, and Janey took the opportunity to say, 'I wasn't sure at first whether Celia was going to find it all too difficult in a new school, not knowing anyone. But in the last week or so she's been like a different child. Far more relaxed and . . . approachable. So she'll be able to enjoy the rest of the term. The summer term's always the best in the year, I think.'

'What made the difference, do you think? Was it making friends? She's always found that a bit difficult.'

'She seems to get on all right with most of the other kids,' Janey said.

'She was talking about a boy called Mervyn.'

'Mervyn? There's no one in my class called Mervyn. I didn't know we had a Mervyn in the school.'

'She says he's the same age as she is. Ten.'

'Perhaps he was teasing her. He could be using his second name so as not to have to say he's just another Paul or David. We've got dozens . . . well, several of those around. Or she might have picked it up wrong.'

That evening, Celia's mother asked her, 'Are you sure your friend's name is Mervyn?'

'Of course I'm sure.'

'Have you discovered what his last name is?'

'No.'

That seemed to be the end of the conversation. The following week-end, Celia's mother asked, 'Would you like to ask your friend Mervyn to tea, one day?'

'I don't think he'd come,' Celia said.

'He can always say No, if he doesn't want to.'

'It's no good asking.'

'Where does he live? In the village, I suppose?'

'I don't know.'

'How did you get to know him? Janey says he's not in your class.'

'I see him in the playground, mostly. Other places too.'

'Do you play games together?'

'Not ordinary games. He can't. He's lame.'

68

'Do you mean . . . Has he hurt himself?'

'He's always been lame. Like I've always been deaf.'

Celia didn't often speak of her deafness. It was interesting that she could be so casual about it now. Whoever Mervyn was, he had helped her a lot, and that was more important than discovering his last name or his home address.

Towards the end of May, the weather suddenly turned cold. There were frosts at night. All the children in Celia's and in her mother's school were sneezing and coughing, Celia among them. Then her temperature went up and it was clear she'd have to stay in bed for a day or two. Her mother worried. They were short-staffed at her own school and she knew she ought to go to work, but she didn't like the idea of leaving Celia alone all day.

'I'll be all right, Mum,' Celia said.

'I might be able to come back early.'

'I'll be all right,' Celia repeated.

Her mother went next door and enlisted Mrs Treadgold's help. As usual Mrs Treadgold was ready to do anything she could. She would take up something at midday on a tray, she would sit in the house, if Celia wanted. But Celia was firm. She would like to see Mrs Treadgold from time to time, and she would love one of Mrs T.'s pot-luck stews on the tray, but she didn't need anyone to stay with her. So Celia's mother went off the next morning, only slightly anxious about her daughter. Celia wasn't really ill, her mother could be reached any time by telephone, Mrs Treadgold would do more, rather than less, than she promised. In any case, Celia was a sensible child. She had books to read and she would probably be asleep for some of the solitary hours.

When her mother came back in the afternoon, she found Celia feeling better and very nearly cheerful. Mrs T. had

brought in a delicious meal and she'd eaten every bit of it.
'How about the morning while Mrs T. was out shopping?
Were you lonely then?' her mother asked.

'No. Mervyn was here,' Celia said.

Her mother was startled. 'Why wasn't he in school?'

'He didn't have to be.'

'How did he get in?'

'He just did.'

Strange. Celia's mother was not altogether happy at the
idea of an unknown boy getting into the cottage when
Celia was there alone. To Celia she said only, 'Is he coming
here again?'

'He didn't say.'

Celia's mother was sure – well, almost sure – that she
hadn't left the front or the back door of the cottage
unlocked that morning. Mrs T., of course, had a key.
Before she left the following day, she asked Mrs Treadgold
to keep a look-out for a boy of about Celia's age, who
might be coming to visit her. 'It's just that I don't know
this boy. I've never seen him. Celia seems to like him a lot,
but . . .'

'I'll keep my eyes open,' Mrs T. promised. But when
Celia's mother came home that afternoon, Mrs T. had
nothing to report. No one could have come to the cottage
without her noticing, she was certain of that. Celia seemed
content and was well enough for her mother to agree to
her going back to school after the week-end. She was
pleased that Celia wanted to go back as soon as possible.
She was pleased, too, that on Saturday and Sunday Celia
had other visitors. There was Emily, dark and lively, who
chattered at such a pace it was astonishing that Celia could
keep up with her; there was Marian, who talked less, but
was prepared to play endless games of Scrabble and
Monopoly and Gin Rummy. There was Sharon, who

brought fudge she'd made herself. Celia certainly seemed popular enough now, her mother thought. But no Mervyn appeared. Nor did the talkative Emily ever mention him, and when Celia's mother asked her, as she left at the front door, 'Do you know a boy called Mervyn?', the dark curly head was shaken, with 'Never heard of anyone called Mervyn. Funny name!'

Celia was back at school on the Monday and the term marched on, through wonderful, sunny, hot, rosy days, through sudden cool spells, through exams at Celia's mother's school, and visits to the local swimming baths, to the river, to local fêtes and other summer festivities. Towards the middle of July, school work slowed down and almost stopped, in favour of end of term concerts and prize-givings. Celia, to her mother's surprise, had a part in the school play. She was still more astonished when she attended the performance, about which Celia had told her nothing, except what clothes she was to wear, to discover that Celia's rôle was a comic one, and that she carried it off outstandingly well. After the final curtain, she joined her mother in the audience's part of the hall for comments and congratulations.

'That was wonderful, Celia! I'd no idea you were such a good actress.'

'I was all right, wasn't I?'

'You were terrific.'

It was reassuring, too, to see how the other children came up to Celia to praise her. Emily hugged her. 'Celia, you're magic!' 'Great, really great!' someone else was saying. 'You were one of the best.' 'No, she wasn't, she *was* the best!' While this was going on round Celia, flushed and happy, her mother saw Janey Preston approaching. 'It's quite extraordinary how your daughter's taken to the school and us. I must admit, when she first arrived in April,

I wasn't sure how long it was going to be before she'd really join in – and now look at her! And it's not just acting she's good at. Her school work's excellent. It was just the first two or three weeks, she seemed a bit out of things, wasn't it? After that, everything happened.'

'That was when she started making friends,' Celia's mother said.

'That makes sense. By the way, I've never been able to track down the boy you asked me about. What was his name?'

'Mervyn. Celia says he's lame.'

'Lame? I don't think . . .' Janey began. Then she was called away by another proud parent, and Celia and her mother began to push their way towards the doors. On the way out, Celia turned back and waved to someone at the further end of the hall, where the stage had been set. 'One of your friends? Was it Emily?' her mother asked.

'No. It's Mervyn.'

'Where? Do show me. You know I've never seen him.'

'There! Up on the stage by the curtain. That's Mervyn.'

But when Celia's mother could see between the heads of the jostling crowd, there were too many people around the stage for her to be able to distinguish one boy rather than another. 'Was he acting in the play?' she asked, and Celia said, 'No. Just helping.' So she'd missed seeing him again.

Mrs Treadgold came in later that evening to share the celebratory supper and to hear the whole story of the production and the alarms and mistakes that go into the making of a play, and which Celia hadn't been talking about till now. Now she wanted to recount everything that had happened, the hopes, the disappointments, leading up to the final triumph. After she'd gone to bed, her mother said, 'I never thought she'd have a success like this. Isn't it wonderful?' She found herself absurdly near tears.

'Nothing to cry about. That one's got a lot in her you don't see all at once. Full of surprises, isn't she?' Mrs Treadgold said.

There were more surprises to come. Wiping away tears that were purely happy, Celia's mother said, 'Yes, I'm just being silly. By the way, I suppose you don't know anything about this mysterious friend of Celia's I told you about in May when she was ill and had to stay at home? He's lame, she says.'

'Lame?' Mrs Treadgold asked.

'Celia says he's always been lame. He's called Mervyn, but her school teacher doesn't seem to know . . .' Celia's mother interrupted herself. Mrs Treadgold was behaving very strangely. She had put her cup of coffee down on the table with a hand that trembled enough to make the cup clatter in the saucer.

'Mervyn?' she said, in a voice only just above a whisper.

'That's right. Why? Do you know him?'

Mrs Treadgold said slowly, 'In a way, I suppose I do.'

'What do you mean?'

'He used to live here. In this cottage. A long time ago.'

'I thought the cottage had been empty for quite a time before we took it?'

'You don't understand, my dear. A very long time ago.' Mrs Treadgold took a long breath. 'We were at school together, him and me.'

'But that's . . . You mean you were at school with someone called Mervyn?'

'That's right. A lame boy.'

Poor old thing, she's got really confused, Celia's mother thought. She said, 'What an extraordinary coincidence!' hoping to get Mrs T. off the subject and back to reality. But Mrs T. wasn't going to be put off. She said, 'He was such a kind boy.'

73

'I'm sure he was.'

'I had a little sister . . . In those days they didn't know so much about kiddies' illnesses. Something went wrong when she was born. She wasn't ever like other children. Brain damage, they call it now. Most of us, we weren't always as kind as we could have been when she got in our way. But Mervyn used to come to sit with her. He never lost his patience.'

'But what happened? Where is he now?' Impossible to take seriously what Mrs T. seemed to be trying to tell her.

'Now? Gone, poor lamb. It was TB. First his back. His spine, I think they said. Then his hip. In the end it was all over him. Nine or ten, he must've been when he went. I know I cried my eyes out. There wasn't one of us didn't love him. I'd always said I was going to marry Mervyn when we grew up. But it wasn't meant to be like that.' She got up from the table, still a little shaky. 'I'll be getting back now, dear. I don't want to spoil your evening after your Celia's been so clever and you and she are so happy together.'

After she had left, Celia's mother tried to make sense of what she'd heard. It must be nonsense. Mrs Treadgold was in her mid-seventies. How could she have known a boy who was ten years old now? No. The boy Celia knew must be another Mervyn, perhaps a grandson or great-grandson in the same family. That would account for the name. What about the lameness? Just chance. Any other explanation was too ridiculous.

It was ridiculous, too, to leave the bedroom doors open and the lights on in the passage and on the stairs that night. Celia's mother scolded herself. Whoever this Mervyn was, he hadn't ever frightened Celia. It was her grown-up mother who was feeling shivery and didn't like the dark.

She didn't ask Celia any more questions about Mervyn.

It was almost as if she'd rather not know any more. She found, ashamed, that she was also avoiding meeting Mrs Treadgold. 'I'm being an ostrich. I'm keeping my head in the sand so as not to have to hear anything,' she thought. But as the days went on and term ended, and she and Celia were free to make expeditions further afield, or to spend hours in the tiny garden, trying to persuade vegetables and flowers to grow on ground that had been neglected for years, she began to feel more comfortable. When Mrs Treadgold invited them for Sunday tea, with the promise of home-made fruit-cake, Celia was anxious to go, and her mother didn't hesitate to accept.

Celia loved Mrs T.'s sitting-room. It was crowded with treasures. An enormous whorled shell with a delicate rose-pink lining. A Russian doll with seven daughter dolls inside. A glass dolphin, a china swan. A Bible text embroidered on linen. Celia went round fingering, picking things up, asking for histories and explanations. Among other objects she brought to Mrs Treadgold at the table was a faded photograph in a gilt frame. 'Who are they? Is it your family?' she asked.

'Goodness me, no! That'd be a fair size of family, wouldn't it? That's the school, my love, when I was at it. Don't you see the schoolhouse, right behind us? Now, let's see if you're clever enough to pick out which is me.'

Celia bent her head and studied the three rows of children, those in front sitting crosslegged on the ground, the second row sitting self-consciously on an unseen bench, the third row standing. The girls wore old-fashioned dresses with round high necks and long sleeves, the boys were in knickerbockers or shorts, absurdly long by modern standards. Sitting in the middle of the second row were three school-teachers, in dresses down to their ankles and hair in knots behind their heads. Some of the children were grinning sheepishly, others were preternaturally grave. All the girls had long hair, some plaited, some flowing loose. Celia's eyes ran along the three rows, then she pointed to a child in a frilled print frock. 'That's you, Mrs T. Isn't it?'

'Aren't you clever? Not much like me now, is it?'

'Your eyes are the same,' Celia said.

'Well, I think that's really bright. I'm sure not many people would have been able to tell . . .' Mrs Treadgold said. But Celia wasn't listening. She was scrutinizing the other faces, searching, it seemed, for something. For what, her mother wondered. Then, suddenly, Celia pointed again, and said, full and clear, the voice of loving familiarity, 'Look, Mum! You wanted to know what he looks like. There! That one, in the front. There's Mervyn!'

Fat Woman in the House

'There must be something wrong with it,' Charles said, just out of earshot of the agent who was showing us round.

'Why? What sort of thing? It looks all right,' I said, and it did.

'At this price? In this district? Ask him why it's only half the price of all the other flats we've seen,' Charles said.

It was an awkward question to put, especially in a foreign language. My French is only marginally better than Charles's, but I hoped I was getting across my surprise as well as my delight that the rent of this desirable apartment was so low. Could it be damp? Certainly not. 'Look for yourself, Madame. The rooms are in excellent order.' They certainly were. The walls were unblemished, the furniture shone as if it had been polished yesterday. There wasn't a speck of dust to be seen. It smelled clean, if you know what I mean. It could have been a house on show.

'Mice? Beetles?' I suggested, trying to convey by my understanding smile that this sort of thing was only to be expected in an old building in the middle of Paris, and would not be anyone's fault. But the agent was horrified. Nothing like that. Madame Legrand would never have stayed in a place where such pests made an appearance. She was a most particular lady who liked to have everything in perfect order around her. We could see, couldn't we, how she had kept the rooms?

We could indeed.

'Why is she letting the apartment?' I asked. Women who spend that much time and love on their homes are not usually ready to allow strangers in to disturb the perfection of their handiwork.

The agent looked embarrassed. 'Madame Legrand has, sadly, passed away. Several months ago. Her husband is not willing to stay here without her.'

On hearing this, I saw yet another inducement to clinch the bargain. Someone had obviously been coming in and cleaning the flat during the months since Madame's death. My unworthy thought was that if we moved in promptly and played our cards right, I might be able to persuade this treasure to stay on and work for us. I hate housework, and this woman, whoever she was, clearly excelled at it.

I made the signals to Charles which meant, 'Let's settle for this one,' and while he was telling the agent that we liked the place and wanted to move in as soon as possible, I said to Molly, 'Won't it be lovely to get out of that horrible hotel? You can have a room of your own here. That little one, there.'

'I don't like it,' Molly said.

I was surprised. Molly is six. She has travelled with us all over the place, and she has always been the easiest of people to please. 'Why not? What's wrong with it? Look, there's a shelf for all your books and . . .'

Molly couldn't explain. All she could say was, 'I don't like it.' And as Charles and I felt that we couldn't turn down the opportunity of living in the district of Paris we liked, at a price we could afford, just because of the prejudice of a small child, we got the whole thing settled that same day. At the beginning of the following week, we were unpacking in our very own Paris flat. Our very own, that is, for three months.

'Do you know, all the linen's marked in coloured thread, not just with their name, but with the date?' I said to Charles in the middle of my first quick survey of the domestic equipment.

'Is it?' He wasn't much interested.

'And everything's put away on shelves which she's labelled. Or drawers in the chest. And she's marked which coathangers are for summer clothes and which for winter!'

'Not quite your style, is it?' Charles said.

'What d'you mean?'

'You're not exactly tidy, are you? You never put anything away at all until I bully you.'

'I'm going to be terrifically tidy here. You'll see,' I said.

'I'm sure I will. You'll keep it up for three days and then we'll be back to your clothes all over the bedroom and no room to eat because the table's covered with your papers,' Charles said. I didn't answer that. Some replies are better made by deeds than words.

I did try. Charles was about right. After the first three days, during which I'd seemed to spend most of my time picking up Molly's clothes and toys, and my books and papers – and clothes, too – and trying to find exactly the right place to put them all, I gave up the ambition to be as 'particular' as Madame Legrand. It was dispiriting, too, to discover that there was no visiting cleaning lady to help me with my good intentions. The surly concierge who guarded the common front door on the street denied all knowledge of any such person. 'But the apartment is so clean! Someone must have been in to look after it quite recently!' I said in my best French. Perhaps she didn't understand.

She continued to shake her head and to say emphatically that no one had been into the flat since Monsieur Legrand had left it four months ago. Did she know of anyone who might come in to do a little housework for me? Light housework only? No, she knew of no one. Here, women looked after their own homes, they did not need other women to come and do it for them. Thoroughly snubbed, I went upstairs again to our flat with fresh determination to reduce chaos to order. I opened the door of Molly's tiny room, expecting to see the usual patchwork of garments and objects all over the bed and the floor. To my astonishment, I found the bed made, no sign of discarded pullovers and slacks. Even the toys were neatly stacked in the big box in which they'd travelled from England. I felt rebuked. If Molly could keep things in order like this, surely her mother need not be such a slut. I went into the sitting-room and slaved till it looked more as it had when I'd first entered it. It took the rest of the morning. By the end of it, I was hot and tired and quite unconvinced that the effort was worth while.

As Molly and I were walking home after her morning in school, I asked her, 'When did you have time to tidy your room?'

'I didn't,' she said.

'I mean, put your toys away and make your bed.'

'I didn't.'

'You must have! If it wasn't you, who did?'

When Molly decides not to communicate, nothing will change her mind. She stared at me, with her mouth shut in a tight line. I even thought at one point that her eyes were beginning to fill with tears. 'Forget it, lovey. Perhaps you did it all in a dream,' I said.

I think it was just after this that I began losing things. Although I'm untidy, I generally remember where to find what I want, even if it's the magazine under two feet of papers, or the shirt that's in the clothes-basket waiting to be washed. But now, objects were mysteriously disappearing from places where I knew I'd put them, and when I accused Charles or Molly, in the way you do — 'Who's taken my scissors? It must have been one of you' — they were both convincing in their protestations of innocence.

'Are you sure you didn't take the filter papers for the coffee?' I called out to Charles in the bathroom one morning.

'What on earth would I take filter papers for? I suppose you've lost them like you lost the sugar spoon yesterday,' he shouted back.

'I haven't exactly lost them. Just can't find them.'

'They were on that sideboard thing yesterday.'

'I know. But they aren't there now.'

'Have you looked in the drawer where Madame What's-her-name kept them?'

I hadn't. I *knew* I'd left the pesky things on the sideboard, where I could pick one up quickly when I needed it. But now I looked in the drawer, and there they were. What was more, I could have sworn I'd left the packet open and the filter papers half sticking out, for convenience's sake. Now the packet was closed, the flap of the top neatly tucked into the slot below.

I opened the drawer of the sideboard where the cutlery was kept. The first thing I saw was the sugar spoon, winking at me with its pierced, silver eyes. I stormed into the bathroom.

'Charles! You devil!'

'What have I done now?'

'Hidden the filter papers and the sugar spoon.'

'Never touched them. I told you . . .'

'Somebody must have put them back. They were in the drawers, where . . .' I hesitated.

'You don't mean they were in the places where they're supposed to be? You're a fine one to be accusing Molly and me of losing things! You must have put them there yourself in this crazy drive to be tidy, and then, of course, forgotten that you hadn't just left them lying around like always.'

It was all very well for Charles to laugh at me. I knew where I'd left the papers and I had a good idea where I'd last seen the spoon. I began to wonder, uncomfortably, if I could possibly be losing my memory, doing things which were later totally erased from my mind. Could I be sleep-walking? No. Things disappeared while I was out of the flat. On several mornings, before taking Molly to school, I deliberately left a cup, a cooking pot, a cushion out of place, I didn't tidy Molly's bed, or clear the bathroom after Charles's morning occupation. Sure enough, when I returned half or three quarters of an hour later, I would find the cup hanging on its proper hook, the pot in the cupboard under the sink, the cushion neatly plumped and square on the upholstered chairs. Once there were even fresh sheets on Molly's bed, the others folded on top of the linen basket. It was then that I admitted to myself that I wasn't going mad or suffering from an early onset of old age. I was being haunted. I was haunted by Madame Legrand's tidy ghost.

I was far more infuriated than frightened. You might think it would be pleasant, useful, to have an attendant spirit who would put away the things you left lying about and generally make up for your lack of order. But Madame Legrand was not only selective in her ministrations; she also contrived to make it very clear what an exceedingly low opinion she had of me, and that she had no intention of making my life easier. She never washed up. She hardly ever touched any used linen, or clothes, apart from Molly's. There I was constantly reminded of my failings as a parent, by finding clean socks or underwear or jerseys laid out conspicuously for the next day's wear, when I had decided that what Molly had taken off before her bath would perfectly well do again. In the same dictatorial fashion she would hang fresh towels on the rails in the bathroom, or place another set of table napkins in the living-room, leaving the used ones in a heap on the floor, as if her ghostly fingers could just bring themselves to cast them there, but would not soil themselves by picking them up and putting them in the linen-basket. She made me feel not only a lazy housekeeper, but a dirty one into the bargain. If I retaliated by ignoring the hints and putting the clean linen away instead of immediately using it, it would reappear in a different and more inconvenient place, on top of a pile of my papers, or spread on the chairs so that no one could sit until it had been removed. Madame had quite an ingenious mind when she wanted to register extreme disapproval.

Before long, she was adopting new measures. Since she found she could not bully me into following her standards, she obviously became alarmed for her treasured possessions. The tiny silver coffee spoons, which I admit I never polished and even occasionally used for measuring out small quantities of spices when I was cooking, disappeared. I looked for them, of course, in the glass-fronted cabinet where I had first found them. They weren't there. It was days before I came across them accidentally, when searching for something else, folded away among the huge damask tablecloths we never used. After a week of angry frustration, I found the very pretty china teapot in the unlocked and otherwise empty wall-safe. The big, heavy preserving pan, which I had nearly, but not quite, let burn dry on one occasion, disappeared altogether, I never saw it again. The drawn-thread-work pillowcases turned up behind the ornamental pediment on top of the big mahogany wardrobe in our bedroom, carefully wrapped in my plastic raincoat to protect them from the dust. If it hadn't been so infuriating, it might almost have been funny, but at the time I didn't think this, I merely fumed and spent time when I should have been working on my writing, trying think of ways in which I could defeat this interfering spirit.

There was no doubt, after the first month, that Madame Legrand disliked me as much as I disliked her. Whereas she would put out handkerchiefs, socks, ties, and sometimes shirts for Charles, and was officious in preparing Molly's clothes, she obviously took pleasure in demonstrating her disapproval and contempt for me. She never touched a garment I'd worn; in fact, she made me feel positively leprous. She did condescend to handle my clothes when they were clean, but only to torment me. She would hide my black bra, my coloured tights, my jeans, anything which she considered unsuitable for a married woman approaching middle age. She had a particular dislike to my scarlet long-johns, she didn't approve of my coloured nail-varnish. Sometimes she would ostentatiously put out the bottle of shampoo, indicating that it was high time I washed my hair. She was an interfering old bag, and a nuisance, but I was determined she shouldn't drive me out of what had been her home.

It was Molly who changed my mind.

Molly had never been a difficult child, and, as I said, she's an excellent travelling companion, adaptable and cheerful. But after we'd been in the flat for about six weeks, she was different. She became demanding. She didn't like to be left in a room by herself, even in daylight, and she would make endless excuses to delay her bedtime at night. She wanted the light in her room left on till the morning. I noticed that when I fetched her from school, or if we had been out together in the afternoon, she hung back as we approached the street where we were living and tried to prolong our staying out. At last I asked her, 'What's wrong? Are you worried about something?'

At first she said, 'No.' But after I'd put the question more than once, she began to cry. 'I don't like the old lady.'

'Madame Tidot? The concierge? She's not very nice.'

'No. The other lady.'

'What other lady? Where?'

She came over to me and sat on my lap, pulling my arms around her. 'The fat lady.' She was whispering so that I could hardly hear her.

'What fat lady? Where did you see her?'

'Here.'

'In the flat?'

She nodded.

'When do you see her? Is she here now?'

Molly gave a frightened look round the room and began to cry. I couldn't go on questioning her. I rocked her in my arms and tried to soothe her and presently she quieted down. But that evening, I said to Charles, 'We can't stay in this flat.'

'What d'you mean? We've got another six weeks here. Nearly seven.'

'It's Molly. She's frightened.'

'What of, for God's sake? Is it the school?'

'No. It's the flat. She's seen the fat lady.'

'What fat lady? What are you talking about?'

'Madame Legrand. Molly's seen her.'

Charles stared at me. 'You're crazy! She's dead. The agent told us so.'

'I know. Molly's seen her ghost.'

'Nonsense! I shall talk to her.'

'No . . . Please! You'll only frighten her more.'

I need not have worried. Charles adores Molly, and he's always gentle with her, and in many ways more perceptive about her than I am. The next day I heard him asking her about her school, her friends, what she liked or didn't like about Paris. He said, at last, 'Is there anything here you don't like, or that frightens you?'

She sat very still on his lap.

'Come on, Molly-my-coddling. Tell me. Promise I won't laugh.'

She said very quietly, 'I don't like the fat lady.'

'Tell me about her.'

'She comes into my room.'

'Just into your room? Or into this room too?'

'She goes into all the rooms.'

'What does she do there?'

Molly said, 'She touches things. She goes round looking. I don't like her.'

'You know Mum and I would never let anyone hurt you?'

Molly nodded, but she was not entirely reassured. After this conversation, Charles said to me, 'All right. I agree, we can't stay. It's a pity, though, that you ever said anything to her . . .'

'I never said a word.'

'Not about ghosts. I know you wouldn't. But about Madame What's-her-name?'

'Not even about things getting lost. Or put away.'

'We'd better start looking for somewhere else,' Charles said, gloomy at the prospect.

'I'll go back to the agent tomorrow.'

'It's such a convenient place, this. It is a pity,' Charles repeated.

That was a Saturday. The very next day, something happened which convinced Charles, if he hadn't completely believed me before, that we should leave for another apartment as soon as possible.

We had all gone out for a stroll in the afternoon. We'd visited the Pompidou Centre, and seen jugglers, acrobats and pavement artists performing outside the vast, utilitarian building. Molly had enjoyed watching them and Charles and I had to tear her away long before she was ready to leave. A French professor, one of Charles's colleagues, was coming to have a drink with us early that evening, and I wanted to get back to the flat well before his arrival. Molly had been excited, chattering and rosy, until we reached our street, when she began to drag on my hand and to walk much slower. We were inside the building, past the concierge's little spy-cubicle, when Molly said, 'I don't want to go up.'

'Come on, love. You're cold with standing around watching the conjuror. Come upstairs quickly, and I'll make you a hot drink.'

'I don't want to.'

'Molly, we've got to. Professor Richard will be here any minute. We're later than we meant to be, anyway. Dad and I have got to get the drinks ready. And I've got some of those tiny cheese biscuits you like. You can hand them round for us.'

Either of us could just have picked Molly up and carried her upstairs. But we didn't want to force her. We must have been standing there for nearly five minutes, trying to persuade her that there was nothing to be frightened of, that we'd all be together, that it would be much cosier and safer up in the flat. At last she was taking a few reluctant steps upwards, when we heard the bell of the outer door ring, and we saw Professor Richard pass the concierge and wave to us as we stood huddled on the first stairway. We apologized, explained that we'd only just got back, then we all began to climb the stairs together. We were on the second flight when I felt Molly, beside me, suddenly pull sideways towards the wall, as if trying to avoid someone coming down on the banister edge of the steps.

'Molly? What's the matter?'

'I don't want her to touch me,' Molly said in a whisper.

'There's no one here, darling.'

But she was shrunk against the wall, pulling me with her. I followed her eyes, looking first up the twisting stair, then down into the stairwell. I heard her sigh of relief as she began mounting the steps quickly, eager now to reach our own front door. There we had to wait for Charles, who had the key. He must have seen what had happened. He cocked an eyebrow at me, and I made the face which means, 'Don't ask me now.' He unlocked the door and stood back while first Molly and I, and then the Professor went into the little lobby. The sitting-room door was directly opposite. Charles flung it open and indicated that the Professor should go straight in.

Someone gasped. Was it Charles, or our visitor? On the low couch which was the first thing you saw as you entered the room, the fat lady had spread out, in what I can only call an abandoned attitude, my scarlet long-johns. She must have gone against her own sense of decorum to take such a step, but I could imagine how she must have determined to take it in order to preserve her household gods from my unworthy hands. And she succeeded. We moved out the next day, back into the expensive and dreary hotel. But Molly was happy again, and I . . . As I sat, trying to work, on an unsteady table, surrounded by the familiar jumble of our joint possessions, I imagined Madame Legrand in the flat. Undisturbed now, she was going round with her duster and her *aspirateur* (the vacuum cleaner), 'touching things' as Molly had said; secure now that no unhallowed hands would desecrate the perfection of her hallowed home. The fat lady had won.

How to be a Ghost

Have you ever thought seriously about what it's like to be a ghost? I bet you haven't, any more than I did. While you're still a lifer you're generally more interested in what it would be like to *see* a ghost. You never think what it's like to be one of us. So now I'm going to tell you.

First of all, there aren't all that many of us who want to come back haunting after we're dead. Most of us are quite pleased not to have to bother about it. We mostly want to be left to get on with Afterwards. And I'm not going to tell you what Afterwards is like. You wouldn't understand and, anyway, I'm not supposed to try.

The ghosts who do want to go haunting, do it for all sorts of different reasons. Some of them just want to go back to places they liked while they were still alive. Sometimes it's so they can moon around and say how beautiful it all was and pretend they're still lifers there. Sometimes they think they want to see how it looks now. That can be very disappointing, especially if they leave it too long. I've known ghosts who went back to their houses or their caravans or their stately homes and there wasn't a trace of them left, it was all tower blocks or allotments or – one lady ghost told me – a supermarket. That particular ghost was sad at first, because she'd lived in a hulking great castle with fields and forests and things, and when she saw it again it was a council estate and, as I said, a supermarket. But she loved it, after a time. She said how convenient it would have been for her, instead of having to wait for chaps to go out and kill rabbits and deer and all that, and for the peasants to bring in the vegetables; she'd much rather have been able just to nip down to the shops and buy what she needed, when she needed it. 'You can't think what a lot went to waste before they invented fridges,' she told me.

That reminds me of the ghosts who really want to know what's going on. They don't haunt because they want to wring their hands and wail about something that happened hundreds of years ago. They want to know about the latest inventions. Sometimes they come back from their haunts very cross, and say, 'If only I'd known about *That*', or 'Why didn't *I* think of that?' But generally they enjoy themselves and they play around with inventions and machines like nobody's business. Of course that isn't really allowed, but once you've got back as a ghost, there's not much Anybody can do to stop you. There was a poet I met, quite young, who hadn't ever got his poems published while he was alive, so when he discovered a computer in the office where he'd worked, he fed all sort of things into it which weren't supposed to be there. When the office lifers came the next day and tried to make the computer come up with some figures they wanted, what it printed out was this poet's poetry instead. He told me they were very cross and they started saying there must be a ghost in the machine. He wasn't a very good poet, I don't think, but it was nice for him to see his poems printed for once. Even if he was dead first.

The sort of ghost everyone knows about is the sort who goes haunting because he's trying to get a lifer to do something for him, like revenge his horrible murder, or discover the hidden treasure, or find a will that's been lost. Those ghosts are mostly angry; they are also what I call the show-off ghosts. They love dressing up. They wear clanking armour, or white sheets with skulls, or black velvet and white ruffs like Mary Queen of Scots. Often those aren't at all the sort of clothes they wore while they were alive, but they think it makes them grander when they start saying 'REVENGE ME!' or 'OH HORROR, HORROR!' and things like that. They act a lot; sometimes I see them practising in front of mirrors, making faces and trying out their voices. What's really annoying for them is when the lifers they're visiting can't see them or hear them either. I suppose you do know that not everyone can see ghosts or hear them or even feel them. Kids are good at it. I've never not been seen by a kid. But for the dressing-up ghosts it just about sends them crazy, after all that bother, finding the right clothes, and often arranging to carry their heads in funny places – I mean not on their necks – and then the lifer just doesn't take any notice. Hamlet's father's ghost was lucky; at least Hamlet saw him, even if some of the others didn't. I can tell you, a great many ghosts go to a lot of trouble, and don't get any thanks for it. It's an unjust world.

There are rules we have to keep. I suppose everyone has to keep to some sort of rule. There isn't anything we can't go through – stone, brick, concrete, wood, plastic – you name it, we can get through. I don't like plastic much, it's somehow a bit sticky, it sort of clings. And we can appear and disappear just when we like, which can be very convenient. But we can't haunt places we'd never been to, which is a bore for me, because I was so young when I died I'd hardly been anywhere. I'd have liked to see some of the famous places, like Rome and Paris and Moscow and South Sea islands and Jamaica and New York. But when you're a kid of ten you don't get to see places like that, so I never will. As a matter of fact I don't haunt much. I did just at first, because I missed my Mum, so I used to go back to visit her. But she couldn't ever see me, though I think at first she knew I was around, so now I mostly stay where I am and amuse myself with some of the other kids who are here too. Sometimes I'm sent on what's called 'duty'. That's for things like looking after babies who've been left alone too long, or playing with little kids who get lonely. I had one really nice job, playing with a kid called Mike. We used to build Lego together and make up stories about the fellows who lived in the Lego houses, and if Mike talked about me, people just thought he was making me up. But then one day, I went to visit Mike, and he couldn't see me. He couldn't hear me, either. I was quite upset. Then I saw that he'd got too old. He was like the rest of the lifers, he didn't need me any more. But it was a pity, I'd really liked playing with Mike.

Sometimes we get sent to fetch lifers to come over to our side. Kids get used for this quite a lot, because it isn't as frightening for the lifers to be fetched by a kid. And we're given a bit of time. You don't just walk up to someone and say, 'Hi! You're going to die, I've come to fetch you.' You have time to let them get used to you. All the same, it's not a job I fancy. I like it better when I'm sent to look after a baby or play with a kid like Mike.

That's about all I can tell you. I don't know why anyone hasn't thought of saying it all before. Not that there's anything new to say now. Haunting has been going on for years and years and years. I just thought you might like to have an up-to-date report. That's all.

Stupid

You can't be sensible all the time.

You try.

Your friends tell you to be brave. 'Be brave,' they say. 'Keep busy,' they say. 'Don't let the other kids see you cry. You don't want to upset them too, do you?' No, you don't. So you try not to think about *that*, you try to turn your mind to ordinary things. There are plenty of them, things that have to be done every day, things that make up the larger part of your life. Things you've generally enjoyed doing. Like taking the kids to school and shopping on the way back, cooking, with perhaps special treats for them sometimes. Reading, playing with them at the end of the day, seeing Tim come home in the evening. But now these things aren't ordinary any longer. All of them—*all* of them—have got little, hidden, razor-sharp edges that sting you, when you meet them unexpectedly, into remembering, into comparing what it was like doing these ordinary, routine things then, before it happened, and now, afterwards. Keeping busy isn't any use. Whatever you are doing, wherever you are, your mind plays the traitor and brings you back to *that*. Even when you are asleep, you dream.

What you can do, though, is to pretend. You pretend because of Tim and the kids. You get the meals ready, you call the kids in, you hurry them through breakfast. Then you make sure they've got everything they need in their school bags. You stand at the door, waving to them as they go off with Tim, all wrapped up in scarves and knitted caps because it's winter. It's cold. You smile at them while you're waving to show that everything is all right. Why should their worlds crack under their feet just because yours has? Then you go back into the house. You look at the kitchen clock. You have spent a whole hour and a half without having time to think. That is good. That is the sensible way to behave.

There's a moment after they've all gone, which could be bad. You used to look forward to the time when the two older ones had gone off and you and . . . But you don't allow yourself to think about that. There's plenty to do. Wash up the breakfast things, make the beds, go over the carpets with the vacuum cleaner. Sweep the kitchen floor. Make a shopping list. You turn on the radio for company. Radio Four. It has to be Radio Four because that will almost certainly provide a voice, talking, and you might be able to listen to words. Not music. Music is dangerous. You can think too easily through music, and besides, music brings back memories. Tunes have a nasty habit of taking over your mind before you've realized what's happening, and of carrying you back to the place, the time, you heard it before, and that is bad. That is not the way to keep on being sensible.

You don't listen all the time to the radio. There are too many noises you are making yourself. The whine of the vacuum, the swish of water in the sink. The screech of the cupboard door when you open it to hang up the clothes Jenny leaves lying all over her room. You're up and down the stairs, too. The dog barks when he hears the milkman coming up the back path with the rattling bottles. But you hear snippets of the voices on Radio Four, and sometimes you find you are almost listening. Two men are telling each other that they are in a wood, and how they are finding insects and the footprints of animals. They keep on saying 'That's very exciting!' You wonder if they are really in that wood, looking for what they call wildlife. Perhaps they are truly sitting safe and warm in a studio in Broadcasting House, just pretending. They could do that, couldn't they? No one would know. Every now and then they say how cold and wet they are. If they are outside, they certainly must be, soaking wet and frozen cold. But it's all right, you made sure that Jenny had her mackintosh, and Jeremy was wearing his new Wellingtons. Anyway, by now they're safe in school, and the building is kept quite warm during this the end of the autumn term. Tim will be in his well equipped office, and you are here, in the kitchen now, drinking your second cup of coffee, and looking at the rain washing the windows outside. You are all cosy-safe and dry.

But she is out there, alone. It's dripping wet all round her and above her, and you can't do anything to keep her from the chill. You can't any more make her feel safe and loved. She doesn't even know you are thinking about her . . .

But that isn't sensible. That is what you must not allow yourself to do.

You look at your shopping list. What are you going to get for supper tonight? Tim loves steak, but it's hideously expensive. What the hell? Why not give him something he'd really like? If it would make him feel better, you'd spend a month's housekeeping money on steak. But you know that no amount of steak or avocadoes or smoked salmon, or any of the special foods Tim used to like, would make any difference to his silent misery. And he won't talk. No, that's not right. He can't talk. Tim has never found it easy to put his feelings into words. He almost never says, 'I love you,' though you know he does. When Jessica died, he went quieter than ever. That night, the night *after*, when you'd both got back from the hospital and were in bed, you put your arms round him and said, 'Tim, talk to me!' But he couldn't. You felt him shuddering with great, tearing, silent sobs, but he didn't say a word. Presently, after a long time, you heard his breathing go shallow and then he snored a little. You lay beside him and let the hot tears run down your face. They were tears of anger as well as of sorrow, because he wouldn't share his grief with you, or let you share yours with him.

Oh, Tim!

The shopping list. Some sort of vegetable. What, though? Jeremy won't eat sprouts, Tim can't bear cabbage. It'll have to be broccoli again. Soap. There's only a sliver left in the downstairs loo. More Vitamin C to try to prevent Jeremy catching yet another cold. He was blowing his nose or sniffing all through the funeral service. Or perhaps it wasn't a cold. Is he going to be like his father, unable to let anyone know when he's miserable? But he's still such a little boy! You must get another box of tissues, whether it's for mopping up Jeremy's cold or your own tears. No! You mustn't let yourself go on like this, you won't be fit to go out into the street. Everyone will be there, shopping before The Holiday. There will be the usual round of platitudes. 'Terrible weather!' 'Are we going to have a white Christmas, I wonder?' 'Yes, doesn't it come round quickly, it's the same every year.' This time last year, we threaded the Christmas cards on strings and hung them up along the banisters. Jessica clapped her hands and she laughed. We said, 'Next year she'll be old enough to look forward to having a stocking full of

presents. She'll help stir the Christmas pudding, she'll be
nearly three and a half.' It is next year now. We'd hardly
begun to get ready for this Christmas before she got ill. But
Tim, who is always early with his preparations, had
bought his present for Jessica. The necklace, the daisy
necklace. He was so pleased to have found it, he knew it
was just right for Jessica. She loved having daisy chains
made for her in the summer, she liked long, long chains
that she could wear round her neck, or little short chains
that she put on her head, a daisy crown.

What has Tim done with the necklace? He can't give it
to anyone else. He bought it for Jessica. It belongs to her.

The radio is still burbling on. Now there's a woman,
saying something about bandages. Bandages mean
wounds, mean operations, mean illnesses, hospitals. You
don't want to hear. But the woman's voice keeps on. It
says, 'We have to unwrap the bandages very carefully,
each one has to be numbered and catalogued . . .' What
can she be talking about? Why should anyone want to
catalogue bandages?

You don't mean to listen, but you find you do. The
woman says, '. . . this was obviously the child of some
important people. The grave wrappings are of very fine
quality . . .'

Another dead child.

'. . . found a great many beautiful objects in the tomb,
laid beside the body. There was food, of course, to keep
the child nourished on its passage from this world to the
next. There was money to pay for the ferry across the river
which separates the living from the dead . . .'

What river?

'. . . and because this was the burial place of a child,
there were toys for it to play with and to prevent it from
feeling lonely. Amulets, of course, to keep off the evil eye,

and a little terracotta bullock and cart . . . a doll, and quite a collection of warm clothes . . .'

She is talking about a child who died thousands of years ago. That child wasn't hustled into the ground and left there, alone, with nothing she knew and loved, no comforts, no messages, no one to hold her hand if she was frightened in the strange, cold dark.

'Be sensible! That isn't the real Jessica, that little, still body, lying straight in the hospital cot,' they said. 'That's only a shell. Jessica herself is a spirit. She isn't there any more.'

She is! She is! That body is the one you knew and loved, that you held in your arms and watched grow. It was in that body that Jessica lived and laughed and cried, with those arms that she hugged you, it was that still shining head of hair that she used to push into your neck to tickle you, so that you laughed too. Jessica was the whole person, that body as well as what people call the spirit. Is it sensible to pretend that you can separate out different bits of a child of three, so that you can concentrate on one, invisible, gone for ever, and to pretend that you don't want to comfort that small dead body which you've so often been able to comfort before?

It wasn't sensible to listen to those voices. Now you know what you should have done.

The woman gets up from her chair in the kitchen. She goes upstairs to the bedroom where there are two beds, but where Jenny now sleeps alone. She opens the chest of drawers, and she takes out what she needs. She fetches a little suitcase from the cupboard in her own room. She looks for her purse. She takes out coins. Paper money will be of no use for her purpose. Two fifty pence pieces, three bright new pennies. She puts the things she has chosen into the suitcase, she puts on her warm mackintosh and she goes out of the house.

She catches the bus that goes past the churchyard. She sees people she knows, and they see her, but they do not speak to her. They don't know what to say. They are not surprised when she gets off at the gate of the churchyard, though they may wonder why she is not carrying flowers in her hand.

She walks along the paths between the graves. There are old, grey stone tablets and crosses, there is a marble angel. The inscriptions on these older memorials are difficult to read, moss-encrusted and worn by the weather. She comes towards the newer graves, where the monuments are plainer, the lettering less ornate. At last she reaches the corner where the graves are few, and small. The mound she is making for is one of the shortest and not yet turfed over. It is still tumbled black earth, half covered with wreaths which are already withering.

A man is standing by the grave.

He has his back to her, and he does not hear her coming until she is almost standing by his side. She sees that his overcoat is soaked with the rain. He is confused. He says, 'I came . . .' but she does not speak to him yet. She kneels down and she pushes the dead flowers aside. Out of the suitcase she takes the things she has brought here. The man watches as on the earth she places a worn, loved-bald plush rabbit; a pair of red Wellington boots; a blue snowsuit; the hood lined with crimson; a book of fairy tales, lavishly illustrated; a packet of chocolate biscuits. Lastly, she lays on the earth the bright coins.

She gets up and looks at her husband.

'In the olden days . . . They were talking on the radio this morning . . . When they buried people . . .' Then suddenly she cries out, 'Tim, I couldn't bear it! Leaving her here alone, without any of the things she loved . . .'

He doesn't speak.

She says, 'I know it's stupid . . .' but he stops her. He steps round the small grave and he touches her shoulder. He shows her what he has been holding in his hand. Then he lays the daisy necklace beside the rabbit, beside the red Wellingtons, the packet of biscuits, the snowsuit, the shining coins.

They look at each other, but they do not speak. When they leave the churchyard, he takes her hand. They ride back in the bus together, sitting very close. In the kitchen at home, at last, she says, 'People would say . . .' He interrupts her. He says, 'We have to stop pretending to be sensible,' and then the tears run, and they stay beside each other for a long time, sharing their silent thought of the child they have lost.